CHRISTMAS WITH HER LOST-AND-FOUND LOVER

———

ANN McINTOSH

HARLEQUIN
MEDICAL
ROMANCE

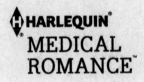

HARLEQUIN®
MEDICAL ROMANCE™

Recycling programs
for this product may
not exist in your area.

ISBN-13: 978-1-335-14970-1

Christmas with Her Lost-and-Found Lover

Copyright © 2020 by Ann McIntosh

This edition published by arrangement with Harlequin Books S.A.

For questions and comments about the quality of this book,
please contact us at CustomerService@Harlequin.com.

Harlequin Enterprises ULC
22 Adelaide St. West, 40th Floor
Toronto, Ontario M5H 4E3, Canada
www.Harlequin.com

Printed in U.S.A.

"Wait," he called, and Elise heard the crunch of his boots behind her, so sped up. "Wait!"

That was what he'd said, just before he'd left her to go to Trinidad, all those years ago: *Wait for me, please? I'll only be gone for a couple of weeks, and then I'll be back, before Christmas.*

Yet even as she'd agreed she'd be there for him when he got back, a part of her was already braced for heartache.

She'd had no faith in his protestations of love, or the likelihood he'd return.

Life had already taught her how quickly and easily others could disappear, especially, it seemed, around the Christmas season.

And Rohan hadn't come back. Instead she'd been told he'd died in a car crash just days after getting to Trinidad.

And she'd believed it to be true all these years.

"What an idiot I was," she muttered to herself, just as he caught up to her near the snowmobile.

"What are you talking about?" It was clear he was trying to stay calm. "Do you know me?"

Ann McIntosh was born in the tropics, lived in the frozen north for a number of years and now resides in sunny central Florida with her husband. She's a proud mama to three grown children and loves tea, crafting, animals (except reptiles!), bacon and the ocean. She believes in the power of romance to heal, inspire and provide hope in our complex world.

Books by Ann McIntosh

Harlequin Medical Romance

A Summer in São Paulo

Awakened by Her Brooding Brazilian

The Nurse's Pregnancy Miracle
The Surgeon's One Night to Forever
Surgeon Prince, Cinderella Bride
The Nurse's Christmas Temptation
Best Friend to Doctor Right

Visit the Author Profile page at Harlequin.com.

CHAPTER ONE

DR. ELISE VAN HAGAN got the callout at seven thirty in the morning, just after coming back in from shoveling the side garden so Baxter, her golden retriever, could do his business. And then, with characteristic efficiency, she got ready and was out the door in just under ten minutes.

This despite the fact it had been ages since she'd last put on her rescue gear, her stomach was in knots, and her hands were shaking.

Tom Harding, head of the Banff volunteer search and rescue team, had been the one to call.

"There's been a barn collapse at Trail's End, and unfortunately Ben Sullivan was inside when it happened. Can you get up there and assess the situation for us? It'll take at least thirty minutes to get the team mobilized, and the helicopter pilot has final say on whether he'll even fly in this weather or not."

A small part of her was shouting she was the

last person who should go. After all, she hadn't been on a rescue for almost a year. What possible help could she render, when she was out of practice and frankly terrified?

But she'd agreed, as Tom must've known she would. She was a doctor and a highly trained search and rescue team member, albeit now retired, so there was never any real debate about whether she would or not. Those, along with the thought of what Janice Sullivan, Ben's mother, must be going through, were all factors that galvanized her to push past her fears.

She didn't know how she'd react if something similar happened to her own son, Jeevan. Knowing the mental and emotional toll his eight-month research trip to Indonesia and Borneo had taken on her, she could only imagine the hell the other woman was going through.

For Elise, memories of past Christmas tragedies already marred the season. She could only hope this incident would have a happy ending.

The only questions regarding her capabilities were within her own mind, and she forced herself not to think about them but concentrate on getting to the site as quickly as possible. Letting her attention wander while she was riding her snowmobile through the gray predawn light and towing Baxter, safely secured in his enclosed sled, could lead to disaster. Especially on a gloomy morning, with sunrise still an hour or so away.

Of course, normally the fire rescue squad would have been called out under the circumstances, but there had been a blizzard in the Banff area the night before. Being on a rural roadway, neither Elise's house nor Trail's End—a husky rescue and dogsledding training camp—had been ploughed out yet. Therefore, Tom had been called on to see if the search and rescue squad could assist, but there were issues there, too.

The team on duty usually assembled at eight in the morning during the ski season, to be on call, so they would have to come in to base before being dispatched.

And if the pilot refused to fly until after the icy mist hanging low over the mountains burned off, there would be an additional delay.

Even coming as close as possible and then riding in on snowmobiles would take a long time to coordinate.

So Elise was it, until additional hands could be found and brought on board.

She just hoped there was something she could do—preferably that didn't involve actually going under any snow.

Instantly the memory came back, causing her to ease back on the throttle and slow the snowmobile until she got her anxiety under control. She still dreamed about it some nights: the roar of the avalanche, the sensation of losing her footing, falling and sliding. Being tumbled over and consumed by the snow. Encased, as though it planned on keeping her entombed forever.

Resolutely she pushed it all back, taking deep breaths, mentally distancing herself from the images. There was no trail to follow, and she had to have her head on straight so as not to crash. A blustery, post-blizzard wind was blowing, too, causing skirls of snow that further obscured her vision and stung her cheeks.

Trail's End property abutted her own but was over a ridge, and Elise had to avoid the trees and deeper drifts as she made her way up the side of the hill behind her property. Getting to the top, she paused, scanning the valley below.

It was still too dark to see much, but almost directly below her was the lodge Janice Sullivan lived in, which also housed the sled dog teams that came to train there. That was already lit up—down to the Christmas tree in the front window—and clearly visible, as were the two blocks of kennels, separated from the house by a field. The veterinary building, which Elise knew was behind the kennels, was a gray shadow in the snow, but just beyond, she could see lights bobbing around and hear voices.

That must be the damaged barn.

Aware of time ticking away, she plotted a path down the hill and set off as quickly as she dared.

As she neared the collapsed building, Janice ran to meet her, and Elise's heart ached in sympathy at the sight of the other woman's tear-ravaged face. Turning off the engine, Elise swung her leg over the seat and found herself engulfed in Janice's shaking arms.

"Oh, Elise. Thank God you're here. Please help him."

"I'll do my best, Jan." After giving the other woman a tight squeeze, Elise gently extricated herself, so as to take off her goggles and then release Baxter from the sled. "Did you see what happened?"

"No, I was in the kennels when I heard the crash and ran out. He…he's buried in there, and he isn't answering when we shout. He had a couple of dogs with him, and we've heard one barking, so we know at least one is still in there."

Finally getting the golden retriever free from the harness keeping him secured to the sled, Elise detached her rescue kit and medical bag. Baxter shook himself, then cast an alert glance at Elise, waiting for instructions.

"The back of the barn looks to be still standing. Is there a door or any windows in that wall?" she asked as she got the disaster response litter off the side of the sled. Putting the bags on it, she grabbed the attached strap.

"No," Janice replied, and they both started trotting toward the building, Baxter at Elise's side. "Only at the front, where the roof came down. It really was just a storage shed, with some old equipment and overflow supplies."

Three men were near the barn, all holding shovels. Two were looking toward the approaching women, while the third was stooping down, as though trying to see through the debris and snow into the damaged building. Something about the third man's posture, the shape of him—even through his snow gear—caused a shiver of recognition, but Elise ignored it, fully in rescue mode now.

"Tom told us not to do anything until you got here," Janice continued as they neared the men. "We were going to try to dig him out ourselves."

"I'm glad you listened. Digging willy-nilly could make the situation worse."

It was clear the front, left section of the barn's roof had collapsed inward, probably from the weight of the snow dumped by the blizzard. As the layers of snow were deposited, one on top of the other, they'd compressed, forming a solid mass. What had slid off and remained in front of the damaged barn wasn't a drift, but more like a jumbled heap of snow blocks.

Anyone under it at the time of the collapse would probably be seriously injured, if not dead. Time definitely was of the essence.

"I think I can see a gap, just there." The man who was bending down pointed. "That may be the way in, if we can widen it."

Elise froze, not from the words but from the voice, at once both familiar and strange. Deep and rhythmic, with the flavor of Trinidad in the way some words dipped and swung, it was one she'd never thought she would hear again and couldn't believe she was actually hearing.

It must be a mistake, a cosmic trick.

Then the man looked up and her heart stopped, while cold flashed sickeningly through her entire body. That icy stream had nothing to do with the weather, and everything to do with the dark eyes peering at her so intently.

It was him: Rohan.

And yet it wasn't.

Not the way she remembered him anyway. Older, which would make sense. But the features she could see—those between his cap and the scarf pulled up around his lower face—were ever so slightly askew, out of alignment. Yet it was so close a resemblance that, for an instant, she was thrown back in time to the first moment she'd seen him, in a club in Cambridge, Ontario.

He'd been so beautiful, his dark eyes flashing with amusement, his smile lighting his entire face. The first time their gazes met, the sexual attraction had been instantaneous and undeniable.

Just thinking about it now turned the ice in her veins to a wave of heat and caused a shiver of awareness to skitter along her spine.

Then she pulled herself together.

It couldn't be Rohan. He'd been dead for over twenty-seven years.

Also, there was not even a hint of recognition in his solemn, slightly questioning eyes.

Even in the predawn gloom, the similarities were so striking that the chance of the two men not being related were astronomical. Now wasn't the time to ask, but she might, later, after having a chance to think it through. Rohan's family had made it plain they wanted nothing to do with her, or with Jeevan.

Some things were better left in the past, where they couldn't foul the present.

Whoever this man was had no bearing on her mission to get to Ben as fast as she could, so she put all the questions and speculation aside, although her pulse still pounded from the unexpected encounter.

Grabbing her flashlight, she stooped beside him so as to see what he was pointing out.

"It looks like a clear space going into the

structure," he said, taking her hand to guide the high-powered beam slightly to the right, to a jagged break in the mounds of snow. The unexpected touch of his fingers, even through their gloves, almost made her drop the flashlight. "That's the side that doesn't seem to have fallen all the way in."

"If the left wall gave way, rather than the roof itself, the trusses could have formed a pocket," she replied. "We need to get a path or tunnel cut to that section of wall, but we have to be careful."

"How do you want to proceed?"

"Let's just get going, Dr. van Hagan." One of the other men came forward, shovel in hand, scowling. "All this shilly-shallying is wasting time."

Both Elise and the man she'd been speaking to rose and moved to intercept the oncoming figure, but it was Elise who stepped into his path first.

Meeting his gaze, she said in a level, calm tone, "I'm trained in search and rescue, and I'm in charge here until my commander arrives. If you have a problem following my orders, I suggest you leave the vicinity."

"Don't be an ass, Trevor," Jan said. "Elise knows what she's doing, and if you muck this up and Ben gets hurt, I'll have your hide."

Trevor seemed set to argue, then just huffed and stepped back.

Elise turned slightly so she was addressing everyone. "I need to take a better look at the building. Baxter, search."

The golden immediately started up the snow pile, working back and forth, and Elise stepped back and to the side, until she could shine her light at what remained of the roof. Besides the conversation among the people outside and the croak of a raven in the distant trees, it had been silent. But just then, she heard a dog begin to howl from inside the building, the eerie sound raising gooseflesh along her arms and making the hair at her nape prickle.

The sooner she could get in there, the better.

Rohan Khan watched Elise step back from the building to get a better vantage point. Simultaneously he listened to the urgent, whispered conversation going on behind him.

"Are you sure she knows what to do? She's doing a lot of nothing right now."

"What do you want her to do, Trevor? Just barge through and risk bringing the rest of the barn down on Ben?" The anger in Jan's voice was clear. "Give her a chance to figure out the best way to get in there. We're lucky to have her here, both as a rescuer and an emergency doctor. If anyone can help Ben, it's her."

Rohan tuned them out, looking instead at the golden retriever up on the mound of snow. It was working along the side of the barn now, picking its way through the hard clumps of icy snow, nose down, tail up, the picture of total concentration.

The crunch of footsteps behind him alerted him to her approach, but she went swiftly by him to where the dog now sat, looking expectantly down at his mistress. When she immediately began to climb up the snowbank, Rohan instinctively moved to stand behind her, although he didn't know whether it was to help or to catch her if she fell.

She went up the slippery mass as sure-footed as a mountain goat, and Rohan heaved a silent sigh of relief when she got to the top.

Something about this woman had caught and held his attention from the first moment he'd looked up and found her staring back. He'd frozen, captured by the expression of shock on her face. Her pale eyes gleamed as they tracked over his face, and for the first time in years Rohan was aware of his scars and had to stop himself from covering the left side of his face. He'd been unable to make out the exact color of her eyes. Perhaps an icy blue, which would fit with the way she'd then shaken her head and turned away, as though dismissing his presence.

It had left him wondering what it was about him that had so surprised her. Was it his accent, or the darkness of his skin? While Calgary was a more multicultural city, maybe Banff residents weren't used to seeing someone like him among them. Or perhaps it was something as simple as her being aware that he was a stranger.

Whatever it was, that look she'd given him had garnered his full attention, and now he stared up at her as she surveyed the building from the high ground.

When she turned and started back down, calling the dog to follow, he automatically held up his hand, offering assistance.

It was ignored; she slid and slipped down the slope of snow, then jumped to the ground.

"There are no breaks in the roof here." She tried to sound matter-of-fact, but Rohan thought there was a slight tremor in her voice. "I'll have to get in through that gap you noticed. Luckily, it looks like there's the least amount of snow there, but we'll have to be extremely careful. This side of the roof is leaning on the snow-pack at the front."

He nodded but found he was doing so to her back, as she'd already walked away. By the time he rejoined the others, she was saying, "Jan, call Tom and tell him I'm going in, and ask about an ETA for the team. You, and you—" she pointed to Rohan and Nathan "—come and help me dig."

"Hey, what about me?" Trevor growled but got a bland glance in return.

"You need to stand back and watch what's left of the roofline. If you see it start to shift or any snow sliding off, even a little, you shout so we can stop. This pile of snow is holding up the rest of the roof."

Under her direction, they widened the crack a little at a time, inch by inch, creating a tunnel.

"Don't go any wider," Elise directed, when Nathan started digging around the edges, probably to make it easier to go deeper. "I can get the litter through at that width, but we have to maintain the integrity of the pack."

Rohan lay on his belly and worked his way forward. The sun was coming up, and he thought the snow at the end of the crack looked lighter, almost ethereal, and realized he was right when a chunk fell off ahead of him, and he could see straight into what was left of the barn.

"I'm through," he called.

"Then back out," came the reply. "Quickly."

He did as she demanded and wasn't even on his feet when she was on her stomach and going forward. She'd tied a rope to her waist, and at the end was the litter holding her bags, but she waited until she was through the tunnel to pull it in behind her.

Rohan knelt to help feed it through, and before it began to move, he could hear her breath sawing in and out of her throat, as though she'd run a mile, rather than crawled three meters.

"Tom says they can't get here for at least another twenty minutes," Jan called so Elise could hear. "The copter is grounded until the fog lifts."

There was no answer except for a skitter of sound, and he couldn't stop himself from bending low to try to see what was happening.

He caught a flash of light as she picked her way through the rubble, then it disappeared.

Rohan's heart was pounding, and it seemed he wasn't the only one concerned, as her dog came and sat beside him, bending to look into the tunnel, too. Baxter whined so softly the sound hardly reached Rohan's ears. Reaching out, he ruffled the hair on the dog's chest.

"It'll be okay, boy," he said, hoping he was telling the truth.

CHAPTER TWO

THE INSIDE OF the barn was a jumble of broken boards and heaps of snow festooning an old tractor and sundry boxes and bags. Shining her light around, Elise picked her way over and around the wreckage, looking for Ben. She'd left the litter behind and was just carrying her medical kit. If she needed the litter, she'd have to find a way to maneuver it through the rubble, and it wouldn't be an easy task.

Getting Ben back to the tunnel in the snow on it would be even harder.

Through the gloom she heard a low growl and followed the sound. Ducking under a partially fallen roof truss, she found them on the other side, the dog standing beside Ben as though on guard. Even from a distance, Elise could see a small pool of blood beneath the young man's head, and there was a beam across his lower abdomen.

She pulled off her thermal gloves and stuffed

them into one pocket, then reached into the other to get the package of surgical gloves she'd put in there for convenience. The need to get to Ben to properly determine his injuries was even more urgent, but when she stepped closer, the dog growled again.

"It's okay," Elise said soothingly. "I'm here to help."

"Do you see anything?" Janice's frantic shout made the dog's head turn slightly, but it didn't budge from its position.

"I found Ben, but one of the dogs is guarding him and won't let me near," she called, as loud as she could without shouting. She neither wanted to scare the dog nor cause any vibrations. "Jan, call and tell them we need a medical evacuation by air, right away."

Just the fact Ben had been unconscious for as long as he had was a worry, and the longer it took to get him the medical attention he needed, the worse his prognosis would be. Gathering her courage, she took another small step forward, but the dog growled again. Louder this time.

Elise did the only thing she could think of, and called, "Bax, come."

She heard the scrabble of claws on ice immediately, as the golden made his way through the tunnel. It was as though he'd just been waiting for the command. If anything could calm the frightened husky, it would be Baxter. After they'd retired from the SAR team, she'd trained him to be an emotional support animal, and he was as excellent at it as he'd been in his previous position.

He was trained to work with humans, but with any luck, he'd allay the husky's fears and allow her to see to Ben.

It sounded as though Baxter was having a hard time navigating the rubble to approach her, if the sounds behind her were any indication. When he appeared by her side and the sounds continued, she risked taking her gaze off the husky for a quick glance behind her.

"What are you doing in here?" she demanded, as the man—whose name she didn't know and had refused, for some reason, to ask for— ducked under the truss and came toward her.

"It sounded like you needed help with the dog. She's one of a group I brought up from Calgary and they're all just shy of feral, since they were rescued from a hoarding situation. She knows me. Don't you, sweetheart?"

He walked by, his shoulder brushing hers, and Elise shivered, both from the contact and the low crooning tone of his voice he used to speak to the dog.

"It's not safe for you to be in here," she said,

struggling to keep her voice low, but sounding furious anyway.

He didn't even spare her a glance.

"Oh, it's not safe for any of us, is it?" he said, stooping down near the dog and seemingly addressing the words to it. "Which is why it's important we get Ben stabilized and out of here as quickly as possible."

She wanted to rail at him and tell him to leave, but she bit back the words on seeing the husky slowly start to relax, ears coming up, hackles subsiding. Bax moved in closer to the other dog, and between the man and the retriever, they managed to form a barrier shielding the husky from Ben.

"I think you can go to him," the man said softly as the husky sniffed at his outstretched hand. "She was scared, but she's doing a bit better now."

Elise held herself back from rushing, moving slowly so as not to upset the husky again. Kneeling beside Ben, she put the flashlight upright on the ground for illumination, then tore open the packet of gloves and quickly pulled them on.

Visual examination showed he wasn't dressed properly for the weather, with his coat unzipped and just a T-shirt beneath it. His skin was unnaturally pale, almost gray, and when she put her fingers to his neck, she found his skin was chilled.

But she could also see the slight rise and fall of his chest, with each slow breath.

Pulse weak and thready.

Pupils—thankfully—responsive, although the left was sluggish.

Taking the C-collar from her kit, she quickly fitted it around Ben's neck. It needed to be stabilized before she checked his head wound.

"How is he doing?"

The low words had her glancing up, and she shook her head. "Not too well."

Reaching under his head, she found the laceration, felt the give of the skull beneath.

"Depressed head fracture and hypothermia, at the very least," she said, running her hands over his chest, then his arms.

She thought his shirt would be caught under the beam lying over his abdomen, but when she tugged at it, it came loose easily. Lifting it, she examined his chest for bruises, gave a silent sigh of relief when there were none visible.

Bending lower, she looked along his body and realized the beam wasn't pinning him down but had caught on the old tractor tire alongside where he was lying.

"Thank goodness, I don't think he's trapped under here. Once I get the backboard on, I should be able to pull him free. I'll have to take a chance on exacerbating any injuries he may have to his legs, but we need to get him out of here ASAP."

"I'll get the litter," came the calm reply.

"Be careful," she instructed. "Try not to bump anything."

By the time he returned, she'd fitted the backboard and pulled Ben free of the beam. There was a definite compound fracture to his left femur, which made it even more imperative that they move as quickly as possible.

The man cleared a path below the truss and slid the litter through.

"I'll help you get him on," he said, ducking under the wood.

"I'm putting a pressure cuff on his leg, and then he'll be ready for transport."

"Okay," he said, stepping past where Elise was working, going deeper into the barn.

"What are you doing?" she asked, her voice sharp.

He didn't pause. "There's another dog in here, probably traumatized, if not injured, and I need to find it."

There was no give in his tone, which told her trying to make him stop would be futile, and she felt a spurt of anger.

"Be quick about it," she snapped. "And try not to bring the entire building down on us."

You insufferable man...

As if he were inclined to linger in a place that creaked and groaned and seemed set to come down around his ears!

But although her tone had him clenching his teeth, he couldn't blame her for being so testy. The situation was anything but cozy, and should he put a foot wrong or move something he shouldn't, he could cost them all their lives.

There was a slight noise behind him, and he turned to see Baxter and the female husky sniffing around. They were both going toward the undamaged part of the barn, picking their way through the snow and debris in their way. On a hunch, he followed.

Unerringly direct, they led Rohan past an old car at the back of the barn, to the second husky.

"I found him," he called, on seeing the trembling animal hiding beneath a low shelf. After a closer look, he added, "He's injured. There's blood on his side, although I can't see where it's coming from."

"Can you carry him out?"

"I'll need to muzzle him," he replied as the dog bared his teeth and gave a throaty warning. "Do you have a roll of gauze?"

"In my medical kit. But hurry. It sounds like the wind is picking up, and hopefully the helicopter will be here soon."

He knew what she meant. Although definitely not gale force, the wind was increasing the rattling of loose shutters and boards, the squeal of wood under unusual stresses. Picking his way back to her seemed to take forever, although it was less than a minute.

After he took off his thick gloves, it didn't take him long to grab the gauze and cut a length. Once back, he carefully approached the injured animal. The other dogs had stayed with the husky, and Rohan hoped the female wouldn't get upset if the male started struggling.

Thank goodness they were in the back of the building, away from the danger of hitting the wrong thing and shaking something loose.

Like the rest of the roof.

He put the flashlight down, where it would give him the most illumination. Making a loop with an overhand knot in the gauze, Rohan got close to the snarling animal and, with a flick of his wrist, slipped the loop over the animal's muzzle, then pulled it tight.

The husky tried to pull away and then, realizing that wouldn't work, brought both front paws up to its face, trying to scrape the gauze off. The

motion seemed to cause it pain; it yelped and
dropped its paws again.

"No, you don't," Rohan said, leaning in to tie
the gauze in a knot behind the struggling dog's
ears, holding the makeshift muzzle in place.
"You're okay. I'm not going to hurt you, and
you know that."

The dog gave him a wide-eyed glare, the
whites showing all around his irises, as a few
rage-filled bubbles frothed from its mouth.

As Rohan gave the dog a quick examination,
there was a clatter from where Elise was.

"Are you okay?"

"Yes," she said, a little breathless. "Just getting Ben onto the litter. Are you ready to get
out of here?"

"Yes," he replied. There was a laceration on
the dog's side, and perhaps a broken rib, although it was hard to tell in the cramped quar-
ters, and with no real time to spend. When it
had railed back from the muzzle it also held its
back leg up, so there could be some damage
there, too.

"Sorry, fellow," he said to the dog, knowing
he was going to cause him pain.

Rohan put back on his gloves before lifting
the injured dog, careful to support him with an
arm under his chest and the other just behind the
hind legs. But it took some doing to pick up his

flashlight from where he'd put it on the ground, and he had to carefully navigate back to Elise, since the light waved crazily about.

Elise had the litter facing out when he got back to their original position, Ben covered with an emergency blanket and strapped down, but neither she nor her light was there. The sun was up, and the room was a bit lighter, but not by much. The only light coming in was through the damaged roof, and with the sun low on the horizon at this time of year, the first rays didn't penetrate far.

Rohan felt a spurt of annoyance, caused by rising trepidation. She'd been hurrying him along, and now she had disappeared.

When he saw her light coming back, and she ducked under the truss, his relief was instantaneous and intense.

"I've cleared a path as best as I could back to the tunnel, but there are a couple of spots we'll have to carry him over," she said, putting the narrow piece of plywood she was carrying on the ground.

When she pulled another blanket from her kit and spread it on the wood, he was puzzled.

"What's that for?"

"For the dog," she said. "There's no way to carry him out, so we'll have to slide him."

Why hadn't he thought of that?

"You're right, of course. But take the wood to the tunnel. I'll carry him that far, then come back to help you with the litter."

Rohan followed her light along the path she'd cleared, and they deposited the dog in a small space next to their exit point.

As they headed back, a particularly strong gust of breeze had them both looking up at the roof leaning above them and made them move even faster.

Getting the litter across the floor was a chore, and Rohan knew he couldn't relax even when they finally made it back to the gap in the snow.

"You push the litter through," he suggested, wanting her out first. "And I'll bring up the rear with the dog."

"No," she argued. "You go first with the litter, and I'll manage the dog. It'll be quicker, and frankly, you shouldn't have been in here to begin with, so I want you out ASAP."

He hesitated, but then came the unmistakable sound of approaching rotors, and he reluctantly nodded.

Getting Ben Sullivan onto the helicopter had to be their first priority.

Yet the thought of leaving her behind left a sour taste in the back of his throat.

She'd bent to pull something from her bag at

the foot of the litter, and when she straightened, their gazes collided.

Gray. Her eyes were gray, not blue as he'd thought before. And something in their serious, gleaming depths made his heart clench and then start to race.

Then she frowned and waved a hand at him, impatience written all over her expression.

"Get a move on. The copter's coming in for a landing."

They maneuvered the litter into the gap, carefully pushing it together, until Rohan had to lie on his belly to keep it moving forward, digging the toes of his boots into the slippery ground to get traction.

"I see it," yelled one of the men on the other side. "Just a little more, and I can get a hand to it."

"Go easy," Elise called back. "If it gets hung up on the sides, it could collapse the tunnel."

It slid through fairly smoothly, and Rohan levered to his feet once he was back on the other side of the snowpack, as Janice and Nathan took charge of the litter. They took Elise's bags off, just as Baxter and the female husky came trotting out of the tunnel, linked by a makeshift leash of gauze tied to the husky's collar. Baxter had the other end in his mouth and led the compliant female out behind him.

Rohan knelt down and heard the board scraping across the ground. Elise had the piece of plywood with the dog lying on it, and she was pushing it along through the tunnel. Thank goodness the male husky wasn't struggling; he was most likely in pain and too afraid to move. Rohan watched it shuffle forward, time seeming to slow, so it moved only inches at a time.

The helicopter circled above, and the wind gusts increased, upping his stress levels, as the barn groaned like a dying beast.

Suddenly the wood's forward momentum in the tunnel ceased.

"Elise, are you okay?"

"It's stuck." Her words were calm, but Rohan thought there was a slight tremor in her voice. "I can't get it to move."

Without hesitation, he plunged back into the tunnel, crawling forward until he felt the edge of the board.

"It's stuck on some ice," he said, panting, scrabbling to get fingers under the board to lift it. Unlike the litter, which had runners on the bottom, the board wasn't faring so well on the rough terrain. "I've got the front lifted. Push."

The wood slid forward, just as someone outside the tunnel shone a flashlight in, giving Rohan some light to work with. He moved back and lifted again.

"Push."

Just as he said it, the sound of the rotors got louder, and there was a long, low creak, followed by a loud crash from within the barn. Instinctively Rohan ducked his head, thinking the tunnel was about to come down on them.

Thankfully it didn't.

"Everyone okay in there?"

Rohan lifted up onto his elbows to see over the dog, and met a wide, terrified stare. Elise's face was pallid, her lips pulled back in a grimace of fear and perhaps pain.

"Are you hurt?" She didn't reply. Didn't even blink. "Elise, are you hurt?"

As though being released from a trance, she shook her head, but the terror in her eyes didn't subside. It made him want to hold her, reassure her everything would be fine, but there was no way and no time for that. Getting out was imperative.

Rohan got his fingers back under the board and growled, "Then push, dammit."

She did.

It felt like an eternity before they were all safely on the other side of the tunnel. By then, the medical personnel were running toward them from the helicopter. Rohan held out a hand and helped the still-pale Elise to her feet. He couldn't help noticing the tremors running through her fingers, but her voice was calm and sure as she relayed to the EMTs her findings regarding the injured man.

Nathan and Trevor picked up the board with the husky and, on Rohan's request, headed off to the veterinarian center with it, while Jan made her way beside the litter to the helicopter.

At that point it was just the two of them left at the site of destruction, watching as Ben was loaded into the helicopter, Janice jumping in after him. The aircraft took off, and they watched it turn, heading for Banff.

Elise sighed. "That's that."

Rohan looked at her profile, able to truly study it for the first time.

Hers was a strong face—square of jaw, with high cheekbones and a prominent nose and chin—but it was also intriguingly feminine. As he watched, she reached up and pulled off her toque, revealing straight, light brown hair, up in a ponytail on the top of her head.

A few wisps had escaped the hair tie and fell along her cheek. Rohan had the ridiculous urge to tuck them back behind her ear. She did it herself, with an impatient brush of her fingers, and a warm shock of desire startled him so much he had to look away.

The sound of the rotors faded, and nearby, a raven croaked.

He cleared his throat before looking back at her, saying, "I should go to the vet center to see what I can do for that dog, but before I go, I realize we haven't been introduced properly. I'm Rohan. Rohan—"

"Khan," she finished for him, before slapping him, seemingly with all the force she could muster, across the face.

CHAPTER THREE

SHE'D HIT HIM as hard as she could, but nowhere as hard as she would have liked. Besides the thermal gloves she was wearing, Elise was shaking from a combination of adrenaline and rage.

Even so, seeing his head snap to the side was highly satisfying.

The shock on his face was even more so.

"What…?" Rohan's voice faded as he raised a hand to his face, his dark eyes wide and gleaming with a mixture of surprise and anger. "Why did you hit me?"

Elise drew herself up to her full height and tilted her head back so she could look down her nose at him. "That was for the twenty-seven years I thought you were dead, you worm."

Then, before he could respond, she grabbed her bags and marched off toward her snowmobile, surprised that the icy drifts she went through didn't melt with the heat of her rage.

"Wait," he called. She heard the crunch of his boots behind her and sped up. "Wait!"

That was what he'd said, just before he'd left her to go to Trinidad all those years ago:

"Wait for me, please? I'll only be gone for a couple of weeks, and then I'll be back, before Christmas."

Yet, even as she agreed she'd be there for him when he got back, a part of her was already braced for heartache.

She'd had no faith in his protestations of love, or the likelihood he'd return.

Life had already taught her how quickly and easily others could disappear, especially, it seemed, around the Christmas season.

And Rohan hadn't come back. Instead, she was told he'd died in a car crash, just days after getting to Trinidad.

And she'd believed it to be true all these years.

"What an idiot I was," she muttered to herself, just as he caught up to her near the snowmobile.

"What are you talking about?" It was clear he was trying to stay calm, but the words were little better than a growl, and when she spun around to face him, she could see the anger simmering in his eyes. "Do you know me?"

"Once upon a time, long ago, I thought I did.

But that was before you and your family lied to me. My sister tried to warn me, before I took off with you that summer, but I wouldn't listen."

"But—"

In no mood to hear any more lies, Elise cut him off. "And now, *now*, you have the nerve to pretend you don't even know who I am? Or worse, actually *don't* remember me? You're a stinking *rat*."

"Just hold on a minute." His voice rose and Elise stiffened, giving him a narrow-eyed glare. "Will you stop haranguing me and give me a chance to speak?"

"Why, so you can spin some new lies?"

"No! So I can explain, or at least try to."

"What possible explanation could you give me that will make any damn sense?" The effects of temper and rapidly diminishing adrenaline were getting to her, and Elise's anger peaked as she realized the backs of her eyes were stinging with tears. "You and your family lied, and for twenty-seven years I've thought you were dead. End of story. Full stop. There's no way to spin that to make yourself look anything but a liar and a rat."

Rohan held up his hand, and it gave her a brief moment of pleasure when she realized it was shaking. "Listen to me. In December, twenty-seven years ago, I was in a car crash and

I suffered a traumatic brain injury and subsequent retrograde amnesia. When I woke up, I couldn't remember anything after the Victoria Day celebrations in May. I was shocked when they told me it was the end of the year, not the middle."

She didn't believe him—didn't want to believe him—until he put his hand to his face to briefly finger the scars there.

Then she realized why it had been so simple to dismiss the thought that it might actually be Rohan. What she'd thought of as differences were actually the end result of the accident— the changes brought on by scar tissue and reconstructive surgery.

As the anger waned and the adrenaline dump took hold, Elise swallowed against a rush of nausea and lowered herself to rest against the snowmobile seat, her legs suddenly turning to jelly.

"Are you okay?" he asked, reaching to steady her as her foot slipped and she grabbed the handlebar for balance.

The sensation of his fingers, so strong on her arm, made her shiver despite her inner turmoil. She pulled away.

"Those months, between June and December, were when we were together. We met two weeks before Canada Day."

They stared at each other, a strange current running between them. Elise's mind conjured memories, many of which she'd tried to forget but still crept their way into her head at the strangest times. Or sometimes invaded her dreams.

She'd held back from him then, even though they'd had a whirlwind summer romance that stretched into autumn and, he'd said, would last forever. He'd made it plain he was in love with her—said he loved her—and wanted to be with her, no matter the cost.

But Elise hadn't believed in everlasting love back then, and wouldn't commit to more than waiting to see what would come of it when he got back to Canada.

Rohan's face was pale. He once more touched his cheek, rubbing at it this time, as though talking about the past had awakened sensations in his flesh that had to be erased.

He swallowed, then asked, "What were we doing during that time? I tried to find out, but my roommate was working as an assistant at the Ridgetown vet school campus, and other friends said they hardly saw me, so they couldn't give me any information."

Heat warmed her cheeks as she recalled the hours spent making love with him, the sense of abandon she'd never experienced before then, and hadn't since. But that wasn't something she was willing to share, so she fell back on the mundane.

"We traveled mostly—to the Maritime provinces in summer, and up into Algonquin Park in fall. We'd decided to take some time off before you job-hunted and I started my residency. We went to places we'd always wanted to see and hadn't got to yet."

He nodded slowly, and she wondered what he was thinking. The Rohan of old had been very much an open book, willing to express every emotion as it surfaced. This was a different person. One who was more contained and closed off than she remembered.

"Who told you I had died?"

From his tone you'd think they were discussing the weather, or he was asking for the time. It was so at odds with the vibrant, sometimes fiery young man she'd once known that the entire conversation felt surreal. She was talking to someone who spoke and looked like the Rohan she'd once cared for, but was, to all intents and purposes, a stranger.

"Your father. And your cousin Chandi confirmed it."

That got a reaction. A flash of anger tautened his face, and his fingers clenched and flexed.

"I'm sorry," he said, clearly back under control. His voice was bland, but she heard the sincerity in his words. "They had no right to deceive you that way."

Then he looked away, his lips tight, a frown wrinkling his brow. She thought perhaps he was going to elaborate, and they could talk through what had happened, but when he next spoke, it was to say, "I... I have to go and check on the husky that was injured. I'm really sorry."

And before she could answer, he turned and strode away.

For a moment all she could do was watch him go, stunned at his abrupt departure.

She still felt weak and confused, and in no condition to run after him. Nor did she want to. What she really wanted was a little time by herself to figure out what to do. Because if Rohan Khan thought their conversation was over, he was in for a huge surprise.

It really had only begun.

Rohan tried to maintain his composure, but inside he seethed, embarrassed and unsettled by the conversation he'd just had.

His cheek still stung slightly from the slap Elise had given him, but he didn't blame her for it. Not at all. She'd been deceived horribly, and had acted out of anger and shock.

Here was another instance of his father interfering in ways that hurt others, and doing so without a care for the consequences.

He'd always been like that—a controlling bully who did whatever he could to get his way. All his life Rohan had fought for his own autonomy, refusing to cede to his father's expectations, or give in when told he would never be good enough. Had the old man lied to Elise out of sheer malice, or as a way to get his son under his control?

There was no way to know, since his father now suffered from advanced dementia, and could provide no answer or explanations.

But Chandi probably could.

He had the urge to call her right away but knew he needed to cool down before he did. Chandi wasn't the kind to give up any information if she felt she was under attack, and once her back was up, she'd clam up out of spite.

Besides, he had the husky to see to, and he was glad of that.

Work, and interacting with the animals, always lowered Rohan's stress levels.

His affinity with animals was another thing his father never understood and had tried to interfere with.

"Study medicine," Dada had said incessantly.

"I plan to," was Rohan's standard reply as

a teenager, knowing exactly what his father meant. "Animal medicine."

There had been threats to cut his oldest son off, refuse to pay for school or anything else. Rohan had almost given in, worn down by his father's bullying, but his grandfather, Baba, had stepped in, saying he would fund Rohan's education. Since the old man was the only person Rohan's father deferred to, it had thankfully worked out.

Rohan liked to think he would have taken his chances on his own if Baba hadn't paid for vet school, since caring for animals gave him a sense of purpose and satisfaction unlike anything else. Nothing in his life had ever given him the pleasure working with the animals did.

At least that he remembered.

The hole in his memory banks, which he thought he'd grown accustomed to and didn't matter anymore, suddenly gaped wide again. A blank space he knew had changed the trajectory of his life in ways he had never really understood, even as it had caused untold pain to himself and others.

Like Elise van Hagan.

He opened the door to the small clinic on the property, used by the vets that often traveled with the dogsled teams. Taking a deep breath of the antiseptic smell lowered his heart rate. Nathan and Trevor looked up and nodded a greeting. They already had the husky on an examination table, both standing alongside it, making sure the animal stayed put and kept calm.

Rohan nodded in return, turning his back to take off his jacket, trying to maintain an air of calm even as his stomach pitched and rolled like a dinghy at sea.

If he could just force himself to concentrate on the dog, on repairing whatever damage it had sustained, his insides would settle.

Yet the image of furious gray eyes, set in that startlingly lovely face, haunted him.

Should he try to contact her again, or leave well enough alone? As he hung up his coat, he pushed the question away, unwilling to dwell on it just then.

As Rohan began a more comprehensive examination of the husky, Trevor said, "Neither of us are vet techs, but we can help, if you need it."

"I think I'll be okay," Rohan replied, just as the door to the clinic opened and Elise walked in with her bags, followed by Baxter, again leading the second husky by its makeshift leash.

"I wasn't sure what to do with this girl," she said, her tone brisk. "Could one of you take charge of her for me, please?"

The dog on the table yelped as Rohan examined the hind leg, and Nathan and Trevor exchanged glances, as though asking each other who should let go of the animal to do as Elise asked.

To Rohan's surprise, Elise continued, "I also thought you might need a hand if you have to operate, Dr. Khan, since Janice is the only certified vet tech here. What have you found?"

She took off her gloves as she spoke, then shucked her hat, coat and scarf, moving with the fluid efficiency he was beginning to think was habitual.

Taken aback, as he thought she would have been on her way after their conversation, Rohan replied, "A couple of lacerations and a suspected broken rib. Plus, it feels like his cranial cruciate ligament is torn."

"So X-rays first, then," she said, walking over to the sink. "And then you'll know for sure."

"Yes," he replied, still shocked by her calm demeanor and willingness to help.

Perhaps it was his imagination, but the atmosphere in the room seemed to heat and thicken. He wasn't surprised at the alacrity with which Nathan and Trevor moved, and once Elise had commanded Bax to drop the gauze tethering the two dogs together, they took off with the husky in tow.

Leaving him alone with the woman Rohan was beginning to think was set on turning his calm, orderly life upside down.

CHAPTER FOUR

ELISE FINISHED SCRUBBING her hands, and after drying them, reached for a pair of gloves. The silence in the room was broken only by the click of Baxter's nails as he sniffed around, and the huffing breaths of the dog on the table.

She'd gotten a little shock of surprise when she saw Rohan, now without his thick coat. She didn't remember him being in such good shape when he was younger. But now, in jeans that hugged long, muscular legs, and a Henley shirt that displayed his wide chest to its best advantage, there was no denying he was downright toothsome.

But she refused to let the thought linger in her head.

She couldn't afford to be sidetracked by something as mundane as how well he'd aged.

"Will you sedate him before you x-ray?" she asked, avoiding looking at him. It had taken all her courage just to come after him, and using the dogs as an excuse seemed silly and transparent now.

Surely he must realize there was something else she had in mind?

But his voice was almost annoyingly calm when he replied, "Yes. It'll stop him from struggling and potentially hurting himself even more. Dealing with half-wild dogs like this is very different from the average family pet, although those can get testy, too."

"Okay. Just tell me what you need, and let's get to it."

When she turned, she found herself under the kind of intense scrutiny that made the hair on the back of her neck stir, and reminded her why she'd fallen for him all those years before.

He had the type of gaze that seemed able to see into and through you, sussing out all your deepest secrets. That hadn't changed in the slightest, although now it was solemn, serious, where before there had always been a little spark of laughter in his eyes. As though, no matter what he saw, he'd always be nonjudgmental and forgiving.

Loving.

That was definitely missing. But even without it, something stirred in her chest, and she tore her gaze away, examining the supplies, familiarizing herself with the clinic's layout, so as to not have to look at him anymore.

After commanding Bax to lie down, she easily found the sedative Rohan requested, and wheeled out the portable X-ray machine while he administered it. There was scant conversation between them, but after the first few fraught moments, they fell into an easy working rhythm.

She had some serious matters to discuss with him, but while he was setting up to operate, or was repairing the torn CCL the X-ray revealed, wasn't the time.

"Luckily there are no broken ribs," Rohan said as he looked at the chest X-ray. "He's obviously in some pain, but the bruising should heal without intervention."

Once they had the husky prepped, Rohan made the incision, and the surgery was underway. When she heard her phone ringing in her bag, she ignored it. If it was important, the person would leave a message.

They worked in relative silence until, as he was removing the torn ligament, Rohan said, "Thanks for offering to help with this. I could have managed on my own, but it's definitely easier with two sets of hands."

"Any medical procedure is, isn't it?" she replied, keeping her voice level, although being in such close proximity to him was difficult. While she could have left, giving herself time to process what had happened, she knew delaying the inevitable wouldn't help.

Besides, she wanted to get a handle on who this new Rohan was, since it was clear he was much different from the sunny young man she'd once known. Getting to know him a bit would, hopefully, give her an idea of how to move forward.

"You said you brought these dogs up from Calgary?" she asked, looking for an opening to ask him more personal questions.

He glanced up at her over his mask and nodded. Being on the other side of the table, with the bright light overhead, allowed her to see the lighter shading in his irises, which at a distance looked uniformly dark brown.

"We rescued them from a hoarding situation. Almost fifty dogs kept in a barn in horrible conditions. Ten of them were huskies, so we contacted Janice to see if she would take them. They need people who understand the breed to work with them so, hopefully, they can find new homes."

"Or maybe get taken on by one of the dogsled teams?"

The corners of his eyes crinkled as he said, "That would be even better, since they're not really used to being house pets, but most of them don't even know how to be dogs yet, much less working animals. The two that were with Ben this morning are, so far, the ones who've adapted best. Some of the others don't even want to go outdoors."

"That's so sad. Do you work with the rescue as their vet?"

"No, I'm a partner in a clinic in Calgary, and we sometimes do pro bono work for the rescue. They operate strictly on donations, so they're usually strapped for cash."

"That's nice of you."

He shrugged, checking the dog's meniscus for damage. "I like to give back to the community."

That sounded like the old Rohan, who'd been vocal about social activism. It was kind of nice to know that hadn't changed.

"What about you?" he asked, gaze still lowered to the surgical site in front of him. "I know you do search and rescue, and gathered you're an emergency room physician?"

The question surprised her. While she was focused on finding out about him, she hadn't considered he might be curious about her, too.

"Yes, I work in the emergency room, but I'm actually retired from search and rescue now."

Once more she was subjected to a moment

of intense scrutiny. "Why did you give it up? From what I saw today, you're very good at it."

"It was time," she said, succinctly. "Also, Baxter had been injured, and they warned me that continuing a full schedule might eventually make him lame, so we retired together."

No way would she talk about the avalanche that had caused Bax's injury, and the nightmares that continued to haunt her. It was the first time in her life she'd given up anything out of fear, and she couldn't help the shame that swamped her every time she thought about it.

The meniscus was sound, so Rohan prepared to drill the holes necessary to anchor the sutures that would keep the bones aligned and stabilize the stifle.

"What happened to you after the accident? Did you come back to Canada after you recovered?"

Rohan's hands stilled for an instant, then started moving again.

"I had to have a number of operations, and some reconstructive surgery. It took me more than a year to get back to normal." He paused, as though considering what he'd just said. "Well, back to a new normal, anyway. Then I got a job as a government vet, figuring I'd stay in Trinidad rather than come back here."

There was a finality to his words. When he

reached for the drill and asked Elise to hold the dog's leg so it didn't shift, she got the impression he didn't want to elaborate further. That he'd closed himself off in a way she knew he never would have years before.

As she watched Rohan's nimble fingers attach the sutures to the bone, she wondered where that man had gone, and if any of his old personality remained.

She hoped so, for all their sakes.

Rohan couldn't stop wondering why Elise van Hagan had come to offer her help, but as he answered her almost too casual questions, his curiosity was further piqued.

Was she, too, wondering what exactly had transpired all those years ago to lead his family to lie to her? Or was there something else she wanted to know?

He couldn't help wondering what their relationship had been like, and if she'd been disappointed when he hadn't returned. If she'd mourned him.

Had he been in love with her, fully and passionately, the way he'd come to suspect he was no longer capable of being?

It was so long ago it felt silly to bring any of it up now, but he envied her the memories. And he was once more frustrated by the blank space in his head, where Elise van Hagan, and who knew what else, once resided.

"How did you end up back in Canada?"

He slanted her a glance and had to tear his gaze from her curious gray eyes to look back at the surgical site.

"I got married a couple of years after the accident, but it didn't work out. I felt as though I needed a change and applied as a skilled worker to migrate here."

So easy to distill some of the worst years of his life into two succinct sentences. Harder though to deal with the residual pain and guilt of his eight-year marriage. The knowledge that he was unable to give his ex-wife the love and affection she'd wanted. That she'd so desperately needed.

She'd begged him. For love. For the chance to stay together. But he'd known neither of them was happy and hadn't been able to see any way they ever could be. It was the hardest, and best, decision he'd ever made, but no one else thought so.

The divorce had caused so much anger and turmoil he'd had to get away.

Mostly from his father, who couldn't stop haranguing Rohan about how he'd brought shame down on the family. How he'd once more been a disappointment.

Thinking about that time in his life brought up so many emotions—none of which he wanted to deal with.

"Okay," he said, dragging his mind back to the task at hand and giving the repair site one last inspection. "I'm ready to close, and then I'll stitch the laceration on his side. After that, we can put him in a kennel to recover."

Elise didn't reply but silently handed him the needle, already prepared for suturing, and watched as he closed the incision site.

To forestall any more questions about the past, he asked, "Are you ready for Christmas?"

He glanced at her as he spoke, and saw a little frown pinch the skin between her brows.

"Originally I was going to work, but HR told me I needed to take my accumulated vacation time over the holidays. Other than the annual Christmas party put on by the SAR team, I don't have much planned."

"No family to celebrate with?" He didn't know why it was so important to ask, especially since her plans sounded suspiciously like his own. It had been years since he'd enjoyed Christmas—so many that sometimes he wondered if he ever had. Yet he wanted to know as much about her as he could.

"None nearby," she said cryptically, and with

the kind of finality that said she didn't want to talk about it anymore.

They finished working on the dog in almost complete silence, and Rohan noticed that the frown didn't leave Elise's brow. In fact, it seemed to deepen as they transferred the husky to a recovery kennel and cleaned up. That, along with the lull in conversation, created a suddenly stifling atmosphere.

When they'd put the last of the instruments into the autoclave, Elise preceded him into the outer area of the clinic. Baxter immediately got to his feet and walked over to his mistress. As she leaned down to ruffle behind his ear, Rohan saw that a muscle in her jaw was twitching, as though she was grinding her teeth.

She straightened, and instead of heading to the coatrack for her outerwear, she took a deep breath and said, "There's something I need to tell you. Will you sit down for a moment?"

Her expression—serious and yet strangely bland—made him think it was the one she used at work when delivering bad news, and he took her advice, lowering himself into a chair. It didn't even occur to him to wonder what she was going to say, as she took a seat opposite him and Baxter placed his head on her lap.

"When you left…all those years ago… After you were gone…"

She stumbled to a halt and shook her head. Then she lifted her chin and met his gaze. Her eyes were darker, smoky gray, and for some reason it made his already galloping heart pick up its pace.

"There's no easy way to say this, so I'll get to the point. You—we—have a son."

He heard the words. She spoke clearly, decisively, yet his brain refused to give her declaration meaning, even as waves of cold and then hot rushed through his body, making him light-headed.

"What? I'm sorry—"

"When you left and didn't contact me, I thought you'd dumped me. Then I realized I was pregnant, and that's when I called Trinidad and was told you were dead."

"Pregnant?" He knew he sounded like an idiot, but the information floored him, leaving him reeling. The only question he could come up with was, "But why didn't you tell my father you were pregnant? There's no way he would have lied to you like that if he knew…"

Her face tightened for a moment, and then softened, became almost sympathetic.

"I did. He said he didn't care—just said I wasn't to call there ever again."

CHAPTER FIVE

ELISE SAW THE emotional struggle play out on Rohan's face as her revelation sank in, and her heart ached for him. Hers was an old, hardly remembered distress, soothed by the years of having and raising her child. This pain she'd visited on him by telling him about his father's betrayal was fresh, and the effects were clear to see in Rohan's expression.

"Why would he do that?" It was barely a whisper, and she could see the shock in his wide eyes and the pallor of his skin. "Lie like that, disavow his own grandchild?"

"I don't know," she said softly, unsurprised when Baxter abandoned her to go to Rohan and nudge his hand. Even though his gaze never left Elise, Rohan's fingers turned to scratch under Baxter's chin. "But you always said your father was manipulative."

"That's not manipulative." Rohan's voice rose slightly. "That's cruel."

They contemplated his words in silence, and Elise wondered what he was thinking, whether what she'd said had truly sunk in yet. Then his eyes widened further, and the hand below Baxter's chin stilled.

"A son?"

It was a question, and yet said with such wonder that she knew he wasn't questioning whether she was telling the truth or not. Somehow, that acceptance filled her with pleasure.

"Yes. Jeevan."

"Jeevan was my grandfather's name."

"I know," she replied quietly. "I named him that because you always said how much you loved your grandfather, and I wanted our son to have some connection to your family, no matter how small."

The corner of his mouth twitched. "My grandfather didn't like his name, because there was an Indian actor who used it, and he was always the villain in movies."

"I looked it up somewhere or other, and saw that it meant 'life.' I thought then it was even more appropriate."

Back then, she'd thought Rohan's life had ended, just as his son's was beginning. She'd been struck by the symmetry of it.

Before she could say anything more, Rohan

sprang to his feet, making Baxter jump aside in surprise.

"Where is he?" Rohan looked around, as though expecting Jeevan to appear suddenly, beside him.

"He's been in Indonesia and is probably on his way to Australia right now. He's an ornithologist and was on a research mission that ended a couple of days ago, but a friend invited him to spend Christmas in Sydney."

"An ornithologist?" Rohan sank back down into the chair.

"Yes. I even have his noisy African gray, Titan, to prove it. Jeevan would have turned the house into an aviary if I'd allowed it, but I let him keep just one. He was a rescue."

Rohan seemed to be digesting all she'd said, his thousand-yard stare hiding his thoughts. Then his gaze sharpened on her again.

"Is his being away why you said you weren't planning on celebrating this Christmas?"

The perceptiveness of the comment should have surprised her but didn't. Rohan had always had the ability to see the bigger picture.

"It's the first time we'll be apart for the holiday, so yes, I didn't feel like fussing."

"I haven't enjoyed Christmas in years," he said. "Not since the accident, really."

She nodded, looking away, suddenly awash

with all the pain she'd experienced over Christmases past.

"It's not my favorite time of year," she admitted. "So in a way, it's a relief not to have to go through the motions."

He was silent for a moment, making her glance back at him, only to have her gaze once more snared. "Because of what happened with me?"

"Partially." It wasn't something she wanted to discuss, and she sought a way to distract him.

But before she could think of anything, he asked, "Tell me what happened, after I left to go back to Trinidad."

She could remember the devastation she'd felt, but now it was distant, and it didn't hurt to tell him the truth.

"You called the first night after you'd arrived, and said you'd call me the next day. When I didn't hear from you for a couple of days after that, I called, but everyone kept telling me you weren't there, or not available. I just thought you'd dumped me. You'd said you'd be back before Christmas but didn't show up. And then..."

She paused, and he said the words for her.

"Then you realized you were pregnant."

Elise nodded and took a deep breath, wondering why that part of the story had been so difficult to articulate.

"I called one more time, and that's when I was told you were dead."

Anger sparked in his gaze.

"I need you to know I never abandoned you. The accident happened the first night I was there. My cousin and I were hit head-on by an oncoming vehicle. He died on the scene, and I was in hospital for almost two months."

He touched his face, running his fingers along the scars, and then abruptly dropped his hand back into his lap.

"I'm sorry," she said, a wealth of pain in the low words. "But I'm glad you didn't die."

All of that was in the past. Now was the time to look to the present, and the future.

So she asked, "Will you be willing to meet Jeevan, once he gets back to Canada?"

"How can you even ask that? I can't wait." His reaction was swift and clearly heartfelt. Then he frowned as he continued, his anger evident. "But I can't blame you for asking, after what my family did. That's the most despicable, horrible…"

His voice faded and, rising suddenly, he looked around, tugging at the neck of his Henley. Elise saw the perspiration that popped out on his brow and upper lip, the sudden, intensifying pallor fading his skin to a muddy gray, and she rose, too.

"Are you okay?" Crossing the room, she took his wrist between her fingers, immediately feeling the racing pulse. "Sit down. Take some deep breaths."

"No," he said, his voice hoarse. "I just need some air."

"Take Bax with you, if you don't mind. He probably needs to go out." She hoped the dog's presence would help him navigate whatever it was he was going through.

Rohan was tugging on his coat, his movements jerky and uncoordinated.

"Of course," he replied politely, as if by rote, already reaching for the door handle. "We'll be back in a minute. Come, Baxter."

And, with a swirl of cold air, man and dog slipped out into the frigid morning.

He hadn't had an anxiety attack like this in years. Not since leaving Trinidad and coming back to Canada. His heart pounded, as though trying to push its way out of his chest, and his skin was on fire. As Rohan strode through the snow, taking deep gulps of cold, fresh air, his mind whirled with all the information Elise had given him.

He had a son, whom he'd never seen, never gotten to know. A child who'd grown up thinking his father was dead, because of a lie told twenty-seven years ago.

At least that was what Elise had said.

Rohan stopped walking, shaking his head. Something about the way she'd sounded, the expression in her eyes, told him she was telling the truth. Besides, if she hadn't thought him dead, why even bring up the fact she had a child with him, instead of keeping quiet?

The need to find out exactly what had happened all those years ago was overwhelming, stifling his ability to sort out any of his emotions about having discovered his son. The only way to deal with it was to contact the one person who could tell him how the whole situation had unfolded.

Chandi.

With his father's present mental state, there was no way to ask him anything, but Rohan was almost completely sure his cousin could fill in at least some of the gaps.

Pulling out his phone, he scrolled through his contacts and pressed the call button once her name came on the screen. Although she had retired to Florida with her much older husband, she should be up. And even if she wasn't, he didn't care.

She answered on the second ring.

"Rohan!" she almost shrieked in his ear. "Merry Christmas! What's happening, cuz?"

"I have to ask you something," he replied without preamble. He was in no mood for catching up. "Do you remember a woman named Elise van Hagan?"

She hesitated, and in that small moment of silence, he knew she did. Chandi never thought too much before she spoke, and if she had nothing to hide, she would have answered quickly.

"Why you asking?"

"Do you, or don't you remember her, Chandi? It's a simple yes-or-no question."

He'd gotten to the snowmobile, and eased down to sit on it, sidesaddle.

"I think I might," his cousin finally answered. "There was a chick on my dorm, and I think that was her name."

"On your dorm?" he questioned. "You knew her from school?"

"Well, I wouldn't say I really knew her *that* well." Rohan could hear the evasiveness in her tone, and the background sounds of TV and conversation suddenly cut out, as though she'd gone into another room. "She was a couple years ahead of me, and in the medical program or something. A real swot if I remember right. Man, that was years and years ago. Why you asking me about her after all this time?"

"I just met up with her today, Chandi. She thought I'd been dead for twenty-seven years. How the hell did she hear *that*?"

He heard her curse, even though she tried to cut it off before it fully emerged, and Rohan clenched his phone so tightly his hand began to throb. Yet, when he spoke, his voice was as cold as the winter morning.

"Tell me what you know, Chandi. Everything."

"Rohan—"

She paused, as though trying to figure out what to say, and Rohan cut in before she could come up with something ridiculous.

"You introduced us, and told her I was dead, right?"

"No, no! Your father told her you were dead. I just…"

"You just what?"

He heard her take a deep breath and blow it out. "I confirmed it when she asked me."

Rage swamped him, and in that moment, he was glad his cousin was thousands of miles away, because he didn't feel he could be responsible for his actions.

"Tell me exactly how it all went down. Don't leave out one damn thing."

Chandi sighed, and all the vivacious spark was drained out of her voice as she said, "A bunch of us were going out one night, and we asked Elise if she wanted to come. She had told us she'd just passed with honors, and we got her to come celebrate." She huffed. "I mean, who gets through medical school and doesn't go party afterward?"

"Just get to the story." Rohan wasn't inclined to put up with her commentary and didn't mind her knowing that was how he felt.

"Well, to cut to the good part, you and she went home together that night. And next thing I know, you've taken off with her to parts unknown, and your father is raving about how you're ruining your life, letting some Canadian hussy lead you astray."

"So, Dada did know about us…"

"Yes, you never hid it. And he was *mad*, sah. He wanted you to go home and get a government job, or set up practice to make a ton of money, and here you were, gallivanting around all 'bout with Elise."

Rohan could picture his father ranting, hands swinging through the air, as though looking for something to hit. It was a scene he'd been witness to too many times in his life not to be able to conjure in his imagination.

"Then what?"

"Then you went home at the beginning of December and got into the crash, and your father told Elise you were dead when she called, asking for you."

Just from the way she said it, he knew there was more.

"Don't mess with me, Chandi. I know that's not the whole story, and I'm mad enough to get on the next plane to Miami and get the rest out of you in person."

"Rohan, after all this time—"

He got up, the same rage that had made him sit propelling him to stand, to pace.

"After all this damn time, I deserve the truth." He didn't care whether he was being rude or pushy. "This is my *life* we're talking about, not some abstract scene from a movie or a book. My *life*."

"Okay, okay." She tried to sound as though she was just placating him, but there was a note of fear in her tone, too. "I wasn't there, but I heard you went home and told your father you were going to marry Elise and stay in Canada. He lost his temper, and there was a screaming match between the two of you. That's when Sanjay came by and took you out of there. He wanted to let you cool off."

"And that driver crashed into us."

He'd never known where they were going, he and Sanjay. No one had said, and he'd come to assume that since he had just gotten back to

Trinidad, his cousin had come by to see him and take him out.

"Yeah."

No doubt she'd be happy to leave it there, but Rohan wasn't letting her off the hook.

"And?"

"When you were first in the hospital, your father told everyone in the house that if Elise called, they were to say you weren't there, or weren't available. I think he was hoping she'd think you dumped her and stop calling. Then, when you woke up, your father realized you'd lost those months of memories and you'd need extensive rehabilitation, and he knew you wouldn't be able to go back to Canada, so he told her you were dead."

What would his father have done, had the memories returned? The doctors had held out hope that eventually they would, although they never had.

Then Rohan remembered how his father kept pressuring him to marry Suvarna, mostly because of her family's wide connections and wealth. For a man of his father's generation, divorce wasn't a viable option. No doubt he'd thought once his son married someone else, even if he regained his memories it would be too late to do anything about them.

When he'd awoken from his coma, Suvarna

had been at his bedside, and had stayed there almost as much as if not more than Rohan's own mother had. It hadn't been long before he was so used to her support that he thought they'd be a good match.

As it turned out, they weren't. She'd been waiting for the "old Rohan" to come back. Their life together had been rocky, with her increasingly frantic emotions met by his stony, unyielding calm.

No one deserved to live with a man like him, and he'd eventually insisted they divorce, knowing she'd be better off without him.

"So that's it," Chandi said, trying to sound like her old self. "That's the story."

"Not quite. You haven't explained why you told Elise the same lie."

"Because your father told me to." Her voice was strident, defensive. "And he promised to pay for the rest of my schooling if I did. Your family was rich, and mine was talking about me coming back to Trinidad to finish there, because it would be cheaper. I didn't want to go back, and get stuck marrying some boy from Sangre Grande, and give up my dreams. You didn't remember her, so what was the big deal?"

What was the big deal...?

Rohan couldn't even answer her, with all that was swirling in his head.

The big deal was not having someone who cared about him, at his side, while he tried to recover.

Not knowing he was a father, until his son was twenty-six years old.

Maybe even missing what it felt like to be loved and supported as he fought for his life.

Something about Elise told him she would have flown to Trinidad to be with him, when he needed her.

But he didn't bother to say any of that to Chandi, because he knew she wouldn't really care. All she would do would be to try, once more, to justify her behavior.

"Well, at least she wasn't pregnant, like I'd heard." Chandi sounded cheerful, as if imparting great news, and Rohan froze.

"What?"

"I said, 'At least she wasn't pregnant, like I'd heard.' There was a rumor going around at school that she was, after she'd left, but no one knew for sure."

"Did you tell my father?" Referring to the old man as "Dada" was beyond Rohan's capability just then. He might never be able to again.

"Sure," Chandi said. "He told me to mind my own business and never mention it again."

He hung up without saying goodbye, the gesture feeling like putting a period on a part of his life that had haunted him in so many ways.

It was then he realized Baxter was by his side, leaning on his leg. When he looked down, the dog was staring at him with such concern that he had no choice but to stoop and hug the animal.

"I'm okay, Bax," he muttered into the warm, slightly pungent ruff. "I'm okay. Or hopefully, I will be."

Rising, calmer and resolute, he took another breath of the fresh mountain air, then turned back toward the clinic.

He had a son, absent at the moment, but soon to return. An adult, with whom Rohan would have to connect, create a bond, despite the lies and secrets that had kept them apart all these years.

Just knowing Jeevan existed gave Rohan the kind of joy he hadn't experienced in years, even as the questions of how to proceed awoke his deepest fears.

After his accident everyone said how much he'd changed, but they couldn't understand just how difficult it had been, battling with the effects of his head injury. During that time, he'd found it easier to distance himself from everyone, so as not to be overwhelmed, and the solitary man he was had grown from that seed of self-preservation.

Somehow, he'd have to break through the shell he'd built around his emotions, if there was to be any hope of a good, solid relationship with his son.

As he walked back toward the clinic, Bax close by his side, he thought perhaps, if he were lucky, the capable and calm Elise van Hagan would be the key. There was something about her that spoke to a part of him he'd thought was gone, but which now seemed merely to have been locked away.

Not that he was at all looking to rekindle their long-ago romance.

Even if she had any such hopes, which he had no reason to believe she did, he'd long accepted relationships weren't for him. All his focus would be on building a bond with his son, and to do that, he'd need to know as much about Jeevan as he could before they met.

That was all he needed from Elise, he assured himself, as he pulled open the door.

But the beaming smile she turned on him, which lit up her face and turned it from attractive to breathtakingly gorgeous, stopped him in his tracks and made his heart race all over again.

Not with anxiety this time, but with desire.

"He's coming home," she said, the gleam in her eyes capturing his gaze and holding it effortlessly. "Jeevan's coming home for Christmas after all!"

CHAPTER SIX

TWO HOURS LATER, Elise waited in her kitchen for Rohan to arrive from Trail's End. The road had been ploughed, and he'd said he'd come by as soon as he felt comfortable leaving the husky he'd operated on in the care of Janice's employees.

Her head was full of plans and lists of what needed to be done now she knew Jeevan was coming home. She'd got another message from his friend, that Jeevan was running to catch a flight and had some tight connections, so there was no way to know exactly when he would arrive. She'd discussed it with Rohan, and they'd agreed not to say anything to their son until they could do it in person. It seemed logical, and less stress-inducing than having him flying back perhaps worried about what he'd find when he got home.

Elise was determined to have everything ready for Christmas before he got back to Canada, but instead of focusing on that, she found herself thinking about Rohan.

There had been no way to predict how he would respond to Jeevan's existence. Nor was she confident about how things would pan out, especially when she'd seen Rohan have what she thought was an anxiety attack while talking about the situation.

But when he came into the clinic from outside, and she'd told him their son was coming home in a few days, he'd smiled fully, joyously, for the first time that day, and he'd seemed as excited as she was. "Will you still be here, when he arrives?" she'd asked. "You could stay and celebrate Christmas with us."

He hadn't hesitated.

"I'd like that. A lot."

"I don't know exactly when he's going to arrive. The message I got was from his friend—the one he was supposed to go to Australia with. Apparently, Moe's mother has taken ill, and he didn't think it made sense for Jeevan to go back there with him, when he didn't know what was going to happen. Jeevan was trying to get a last-minute ticket, which could mean they route him through half of Asia before he gets to Vancouver."

Rohan had sat in one of the chairs, still smiling. "Doesn't matter to me how long he takes to get here, I'm just happy I'm able to meet him sooner than expected. I'll have to book a hotel room, though. I'd told Janice I'd leave today, and she has a sled team arriving tomorrow. Between that and Ben being in hospital, I don't want to be an additional problem."

"You might have a problem finding a room at this time of year. Banff's really popular at Christmas. I have a spare room, though. Why don't you come and stay at my place?"

He'd hesitated, then said, "I wouldn't want to impose."

"No imposition," she'd replied, keeping her voice brisk and matter-of-fact.

He'd slanted her a glance, and then, when she thought he wasn't going to reply, he'd said, "I'd like that. Thank you."

"Of course," she'd joked, ridiculously light-hearted at his agreement. "You'll have to put up with Titan, the African gray, and his squawking."

"I'm used to it," he'd said casually, rubbing the side of his face. "I have a macaw, and she's a chatterer, too."

"I guess the apple didn't fall far from the tree, then."

The grin he'd sent her had her heart racing. *There*. There was Rohan.

The devil-may-care smile that showed he had

the world by the tail and wasn't afraid to tweak that appendage whenever he wanted.

"I guess not."

She'd grinned in return, and the unwanted trickle of awareness she felt when his smile widened had made her look away.

"I pulled up some pictures on my phone," she'd told him, unlocking the screen as she spoke. "But, of course, at home I have many more of him when he was young."

She'd handed him the phone and seen the way his eyes tracked across the screen, as though trying to see every small detail of each picture he looked at.

"He looks like me," he'd said softly.

"A lot," she'd confirmed, her heart melting at the yearning set of his face. "It'll be wonderfully strange to see the two of you together."

"What is he like?"

Warm fondness had flooded her as she sought the right way to describe their son. It was so hard to be objective, but she felt she owed Rohan all the honesty she could muster. At least on this topic.

"He was a scoundrel and hell-raiser as a child. I never knew what he was going to get up to next. But at the same time, he could be just this quiet, sweet little boy. For a while I wasn't sure how he'd turn out, and I worried about that all the time. One minute he was skateboarding with his friends, and I was hearing stories about the mischief they were getting up to, the next I'd find him crying over a dead bird he'd found in the garden."

She'd paused, and Rohan's gaze had lifted to hers, stealing her breath for an instant. Forcing a deep inhale, she'd cleared her throat before continuing.

"But as he grew, I realized it would be okay. He's good people, and I like him as much as love him, and I know not every parent gets to say that about their children, so I'm happy."

Rohan had nodded without comment, just looking back down at the phone, and she'd been acutely aware of all she hadn't said.

He not only looks a lot like you, but in so many little ways he reminds me of you. The way he walks, his wide grin. How he so easily connects to other people, even with just a smile or a few well-chosen words.

For all his life, Elise had watched Jeevan grow more and more like his father, or how his father had been when she first knew him, and she'd been fiercely glad. Rohan had been the kind of man she wanted her son to become: kind, considerate, easygoing, but still strong and always ready to stand up for what was right.

It was left to be seen how much of that man

still existed under the stern, contained exterior Rohan now wore so easily.

Then he'd surprised her again, by asking, "Since you have such a short time to get ready for Christmas, and I'll be at your place anyway, can I help with anything?"

There'd been no hesitancy in his voice, but he'd lifted his hand briefly to his cheek again, making her think he wasn't as calm as he seemed. That one gesture made her not want to refuse.

Besides, against her best intentions, she was looking forward to spending more time with him—getting to know the new Rohan better.

"I'd appreciate it, actually, since usually by now I'd have everything done, and this year I haven't even started. But I have a few things I have to take care of, as well as the Christmas prep, so we'll have to coordinate."

He'd raised his eyebrows. "I don't mind tagging along, if I won't be in the way." The corner of his mouth quirked, and he admitted, "I volunteered to bring the huskies up to Trail's End to get away from the Christmas fuss, so it's not as though I'm needed here, or anywhere else. Nathan can keep an eye on the husky we operated on this morning and call me if needs be."

"I have an appointment at half past twelve,

so if you can come down, we can leave from my place."

Which was how she found herself walking out to his car dressed like one of Santa's elves, with Baxter behind her wearing a pair of reindeer antlers.

When she'd got Baxter's harness fastened in the back seat, she got into the truck to see Rohan's eyebrows up at his hairline and his lips twitching, as though he were trying his best not to laugh.

"I'm due at the nursing home with Baxter, and then I thought we could pick up a Christmas tree before we go back to the house and then you can help me decorate."

"Why are you going to the nursing home?" he asked as she fastened her seat belt.

As he put the SUV in gear, she told him, "After Bax and I retired from search and rescue, I decided to train him as an emotional support animal. I didn't want him to get bored and fat just sitting around the house all the time."

"Ah. That's why you told me to take him out with me earlier, because you knew I was having…problems with what we were discussing."

She slid him a glance, found him staring resolutely through the windscreen, his jaw tight.

Why couldn't he even say the words *anxi-*

ety attack? Did he think it made him weak to have them?

Not feeling it was appropriate to press him on it, she replied, "And why I called him into the barn when the husky was guarding Ben. I thought he might be able to calm her down."

"You were right." His voice sounded less stiff, but he lifted his hand to briefly touch his cheek. "And Bax and that female husky led me right to the other, injured dog. Do you think the husky might be trainable as a search and rescue dog?"

Elise frowned, considering it. "Huskies aren't usually trained for that. Her dominant skill sets may not be appropriate, but that's a question Tom, the volunteer SAR captain, would be better able to answer."

"How did you get into search and rescue anyway? Being an ER doctor wasn't exciting enough for you?"

"It was something I'd been interested in since I was a child. I never really wanted to study medicine, but my mother insisted. Once I got into it, I wanted to be where the action was, so emerge was the best fit."

He made a sound in the back of his throat, and she interpreted it as one of amusement when he asked, "A thrill seeker, huh?"

She snorted, then had to smile at the inelegant sound. "I guess you could put it that way. All I wanted to do was search and rescue, but Mom kept at me until I agreed to her plan. She was of the opinion it was too dangerous, and not a job for a woman. Besides, by then she was sick, and I know she wanted to make sure I would be able to take care of myself after she was gone, so I went along with it."

"Did I ever meet your mother or your father, back when we were together?"

He was trying to sound casual, as though just making conversation, but she got the impression he was trying to fill in the blank spot in his brain with facts, since the memories were gone. It made her wonder how he'd coped after the accident, when no one could, or would, offer him any lifeline to his immediate past.

"No," she said quietly. "You never met any of my family. By then both my parents were gone, and my sister was in Calgary, where my mother's family originally came from."

"Is she still living there?"

"No. She and her husband moved to BC a few years ago. Make a turn here."

He put on his indicator and made the turn into Banff. The ploughs had been busy, and downtown was already filled with people shopping and enjoying the crisp, late-morning air. Not wanting to talk about her family any more, Elise searched for another, less painful topic.

"I used to bring Bax to the home in the afternoons, but the residents requested that he come earlier. At first, I thought it was because they weren't as tired as they were closer to the end of the day, then I realized it's because they like to sneak him little bits of their lunches. I have to keep a sharp eye on them."

Rohan chuckled, and for some reason the sound went straight to her heart.

Had she heard him laugh, even once, all day? She didn't think so.

"There you were, training him so he wouldn't get bored and fat, not realizing the danger of becoming obese would come with the new job."

"Exactly," she replied, letting amusement color her voice as she directed him into the nursing home parking lot.

When he'd parked, and she was unbuckling her seat belt and gathering up the bag of gifts she'd brought, Rohan exited the vehicle ahead of her and let Bax out the back door. As they met at the front of the vehicle, he held out the leash for her to take. Neither of them was wearing gloves, and as her fingers brushed his, a sweet tingle of awareness rushed through her.

Before she could make sense of it, Rohan's hand closed over hers, and he said, "I have one more question, and I hope you don't mind me asking."

She raised her eyebrows, trying to pretend his touch wasn't giving her goose bumps.

"Why did you give up search and rescue, really?"

Tugging her hand free, she set off for the lobby door, saying over her shoulder, "That's a story for another day."

Knowing full well that if she had her way, that day would never come.

As they walked into the home and were greeted with cries of welcome, she saw Rohan retreat to a spot against the wall, his stoic mien firmly in place. As Elise allowed Baxter to work the room, greeting all the residents, Rohan stayed to one side, watching. But as she well knew, no one visiting was allowed to remain aloof for very long.

"Who is that young man?" Mrs. Ferguson waved at him. "Come here. You remind me so much of someone, but I can't think of who it is."

"I think he looks like Elise's son," Mrs. Durrant said. "Do you remember, Ada, when he came with her to visit?"

"Oh, yes," Mrs. Ferguson said, peering at Rohan over her glasses. "That's right."

"He looks like Jeevan, because Rohan is his father."

Elise didn't even hesitate. The words flowed

from her lips so easily even she was a little taken aback by it.

And then she met Rohan's gaze, and his expression was one of mingled wonder and surprise. Then it morphed into something else—something hot and wild—which caused desire to flash through her so hard and fast she had to turn away so he wouldn't see it reflected in her eyes.

It reminded her of how, even as she'd kept an emotional distance from him all those years ago, he'd been able to turn her inside out with lust with just a look or a single touch. He was the only man who'd made her mindless with need. Who'd made her forget just why love wouldn't be something she counted on to be happy.

No. No. No.

They weren't going there. This chance meeting had nothing to do with what they'd once shared, beyond the fact that it had produced Jeevan.

The only thing that mattered was uniting father and son, and she refused to allow echoes of the past to muddy the waters.

Especially not the kind of echoes that made her want to tumble into Rohan's arms the way she used to, and allow him to set her ablaze.

CHAPTER SEVEN

By the time they left the nursing home, Rohan couldn't believe how much fun he'd had.

Watching Bax work had been a treat as he allowed himself to be petted, hugged and kissed by resident after resident. He'd delivered little presents to each person, carried in a basket he proudly held in his mouth, and his tail had hardly stopped fanning the air.

At the end, Rohan was happy to escape the old ladies' interrogations, and had tagged along with Elise and Bax while they went to visit a resident who'd been bedridden for a few weeks.

"He fell and broke his hip," Elise explained. "And, as it is for many patients with dementia, the hospital stay caused a marked deterioration in his mental acuity. Mr. Robson is almost completely nonverbal now, except when he sees Bax."

It had sounded so much like what he'd found the last time he visited his father that Rohan was tempted to wait for them outside the room. But the nurse had held the door open for him, and by then it was too late to avoid going through without it being obvious.

Despite his misgivings and the lingering sense of being thrust into a situation he felt unequal to handle, he couldn't help being touched as he watched Bax interact with Mr. Robson. On opening his eyes and seeing the dog next to his bed, the elderly man's face had lit up, his trembling hand reaching out. Bax had shifted, putting his head in the proper position to be petted, and then, on Elise's command, he'd placed his paws on the rail at the side of the bed so he was face-to-face with the patient.

"Oh, you beauty," the old man had breathed, his voice little better than a sigh. "You gorgeous boy. You've come to see old George again. I love you. I love you."

That moment, Rohan knew, would stay with him for a very long time. He'd always known and accepted that animals had healing qualities, but seeing it displayed so clearly moved him deeply.

But the experience that lingered even stronger in his mind was when Elise had, so calmly and matter-of-factly, named him as her child's father.

Hearing her do so had caused his heart to stutter, warmth to fill his chest. The emotions released had swamped him, threatening to drown him in joy so intense it was frightening.

And in that instant, she was even more beautiful to him than she'd been before.

He'd even imagined that something special and wonderful had passed between them as their eyes met, but now he dismissed the thought. She was intelligent, kind and beautiful. Everything any man could want or need, but he had nothing to offer in return.

Not when his emotions were so stunted, and almost impossible to process.

The focus needed to stay squarely on Jeevan. Although his son was no longer a child, as parents it was their obligation to ensure that Rohan's meeting with him went smoothly.

There was no room for error, nor for complications, like his growing attraction to his son's mother.

After his accident he'd been told over and over how different he was, how he was no longer the young man people knew and loved. The changes had been pointed out in detail. How solemn he'd become, how he lacked the laughter and joking ways of his youth. He'd been unable to give affection easily, locked in a cycle of simply trying to survive the effects of his head injury, and it had shown in how he treated those around him.

Elise would remember that younger man, and perhaps even now wondered at the transformation. He had no urge to hear those kinds of comments again, especially not from a woman he now knew he would be forever tied to.

"Okay," Elise said briskly once they were back in the SUV, breaking him out of his not-so-happy thoughts. "Let's go get a tree, and then head back to my place. I was thinking of going by the hospital to see Ben, if they're allowing him visitors, but I refuse to go there dressed like an elf."

Her stout declaration amused him. "But you'll go tree shopping like that?"

"Downtown Banff is Christmas central. No one will even bat an eye. But I'd hear about it for years if the staff at the hospital see me like this."

He wouldn't blame anyone for mentioning the outfit. He'd been trying to ignore just how snugly it fit her athletic form, and how the tail of her tunic swung enticingly when she walked. Her body was toned, but with womanly curves he longed to put his hands on. Soft, round breasts beneath her clingy costume showcased a still-narrow waist, which then flared into rounded hips.

The maturity of her figure was a turn-on he couldn't ignore, especially when she walked ahead of him, bottom swinging with each long, confident stride.

Not even the funny shoes and hat made her look anything less than completely desirable.

The tree market was busy, but Rohan appreciated the swiftness with which Elise made a decision, and it wasn't long before they were back on the road, heading to her house.

"We'll get the tree set up, and then cut some branches before getting the decorations out of storage." Rohan got the impression she was mentally running down an already prepared list. "This evening, if you're up for it, I'll need to do some food and gift shopping. We could go by the hospital then, too."

"Sounds like a plan," he agreed, settling back, trying to ease the tension out of his shoulders.

When they stopped at an intersection, Elise pulled off the elf hat, and once more he saw a few wisps of hair escape her bun. Without thought, he gently swept them back, tucking them behind her ear. She didn't say anything but slanted him a quick glance, and he silently cursed the impulse that had made him touch her so intimately.

He'd have to watch himself going forward, to make sure he didn't do anything else like that.

Bax whined from the back seat, and Elise turned to say, "Yep, almost home, boy."

Her house was a neat bungalow, which, with all the snow they'd had the previous night, seemed to be floating on a sea of white. One side had been cleared, the driveway and walk shoveled, making paths through drifts three feet high in spots. She directed him to park near the garage door.

While Baxter found a spot that needed watering, they wrestled the tree out of the SUV, and then they all went inside.

In the kitchen, they stopped to take off their shoes while Baxter made a beeline for his water bowl. Obviously, cheering up the elderly was thirsty work.

"Help yourself to a drink, if you like, and go on through to the living room." She pointed him to an archway on the other side of the kitchen as she walked toward a hallway. "I'm just going to change out of this costume."

He took a moment to look around. It was no surprise to him that everything was tidy, spic-and-span. Elise struck him as a person who probably wouldn't abide too much clutter.

"Bax! Bax! Mom wants you!"

The squawk of a parrot drew him into the living room, and he saw the African gray in its cage first. Then, as he started to cross the room to take a closer look, he realized the room was filled with photographs. They were on the walls, on the shelves surrounding the television, the mantelpiece—everywhere—and that became more interesting and important to Rohan just then.

On suddenly shaky legs, he moved closer to look at them. Most were of Jeevan in different settings, with a few of Elise thrown in. A chronicle of Jeevan's life, from him as a baby, round, damp and sandy, a lake or ocean in the background, to some of him at university graduation. One of Elise, proudly wearing her search and rescue uniform, Baxter at her side. And then, on the wall, Rohan came face-to-face with himself.

It looked like an autumn day, with a wash of orange, red and yellow leaves forming a backdrop to his face. He was laughing, head thrown back, sunlight glinting in his smiling eyes.

The only thing he recognized in the picture was the scarf around his throat. It was covered in smiley faces, and he'd worn it all through college, been teased about it numerous times.

Intellectually, he knew it was his face, and was touched that Elise had kept his image in front of his son's eyes all those years, but the person in the picture was, deep inside, a stranger to him.

"Who were you?"

He said it aloud to the photo, struggling not to let the doubts and fears overtake him and cause him to botch this important moment in his life, as he knew they had done at other times.

Unable to bear looking at it anymore, he turned away and drew in a deep breath. Blowing it out, he straightened his spine.

Seeing the pictures brought the wonder of it back.

He was a father. Had a son.

A son named after his beloved Baba, the grandfather who'd taught him how to be a man and a decent human being.

Your father thinks prestige is the most important thing in life, Rohan, but he's wrong. And money isn't important, either. What is important is that you do the right thing, always, and bring joy to others. Only then can you be truly happy.

Remembering Baba's words brought calm, and a new resolve to make this work.

He'd doubted his ability to love, to care deeply for another, but already he knew he'd do anything for his son and fight to the death anyone else who tried to come between them again.

Elise stood in the doorway, watching Rohan examine the pictures on the wall, knowing he hadn't noticed her and glad for it.

Now she could clearly see the emotions, as though the only time he could let them free was when he was alone. She'd seen sorrow, joy, confusion, tenderness, and her heart ached for him, even as her body insisted on reminding her how sexy he was.

Being around Rohan—even this new, different Rohan—was doing crazy things to her equilibrium.

When he'd brushed the hair back from her cheek, his fingers warm against her skin, she was transported back in time. The intervening years fell away, as though they'd never existed, leaving her feeling like that young, carefree girl who'd desired him beyond reason.

"Why doesn't your hair ever stay where you put it?"

He'd slicked her hair off her cheek, tucking the strands securely behind her ear.

"It's because it's so fine and straight. Nothing keeps it in place for long."

"You know what? I like that it flops around like that."

"Flops around?" She'd feigned annoyance. "And why on earth would you like that?"

He'd moved closer, nuzzling her so his breath rushed, warm and exciting, over her cheek, as he replied, "Because it's one more reason to touch you."

He raised his hand, not to his face this time,

but to the back of his head, and once more memories swamped her, brought on by the cowlick at his nape. How many times had she swirled her finger through it, or snuck up behind him and kissed him just there? Too many to count, but she remembered as if it were yesterday. And when Jeevan was born with a full head of hair, and she'd seen the same swirl of baby-fine hair at his nape, it had brought her to tears.

Elise drew a long breath into her lungs and held it for a beat before letting it out silently.

This wasn't then, and she wasn't that relatively naive twenty-six-year-old, she reminded herself stoutly. And Rohan Khan wasn't the man she'd fallen for and mourned. They'd both been changed, fundamentally, by the events of that year and all the intervening ones. Now the best they could hope for was to find some way to co-parent so no one got hurt.

Especially Jeevan.

She stepped into the room, drawing his attention. As though watching a curtain fall, she saw the expression leave his face, and it hurt her more than it should.

"Do you have a tree stand?" he asked, as though that was the most important thing in the world.

"I'll get it," she replied, turning away so he couldn't see her silly pain.

As they were cutting boughs and putting them on the sled, Rohan said, "So Jeevan is an ornithologist, huh? Couldn't get him to choose veterinary medicine?"

Elise chuckled. "He swung between the two for a while, but birds were always fascinating to him, although I never really understood it. I don't mind them, but he was obsessed. Made it easy to buy him gifts, though, which isn't always the case as a parent."

Rohan glanced over, and his eyes were smiling. "Never thought he'd go into human medicine?"

Elise gave a decisive shake of her head. "No. Never. He worked at the hospital, to get his volunteer hours in for school, and he hated having to be inside all the time and complained that there were too many 'crotchety old people' to interact with."

That made Rohan chuckle.

"I'd feel the same way," he said, amusement still evident in his voice. "Although I mostly do small animal work now, some of my favorite jobs are when I get called out to do house calls at farms or ranches. A few weeks ago, I had to attend on a birth at an alpaca farm. Mind you, I would have preferred if it were summer, but, hey, at least it got me out of the office."

"I love working in the emergency room—

"Do you need a hand with getting it out?"

"Not right now," she called back to him, although his superior height would have been useful in getting at it on the top shelf.

Carrying a chair over to the storage closet, she climbed up to get the stand, glad for a few minutes to herself.

"I could have gotten that for you."

She'd been so lost in thought she hadn't heard him come in, and the suddenness of his voice behind her startled her into spinning around and she toppled from the chair.

Rohan caught her, bending over her to shield her from the cascade of wrapping paper and boxes that came down around them.

"Are you all right?" he asked, slowly straightening, although his arms remained around her. She told herself to move, to step back, but her head filled with his scent, and her entire body awoke, tingling and heating.

How can he still smell the same?

"Elise?"

His voice was cool and controlled, and she was made aware of how stupid she was being, getting lost in memories of a time so long gone it could have been a different life.

"I'm fine," she said, stepping back and having to suppress a shiver of sudden cold. "The tree stand is right there. Thank God it didn't fall on one of our heads."

Although, she thought as he easily pulled the article in question down, it might have knocked some sense into her, if hers was the head in question.

CHAPTER EIGHT

THE AFTERNOON FLEW by and ended up being a lot more fun than Elise had anticipated. Once they had the tree set up, they put back on their outdoor clothes and went to the woodlot to cut branches to decorate the house.

"Jeevan and I usually decorate the tree together," she explained when Rohan asked about ornaments. "But there's still lots to do. I like to have fresh pine boughs above the cupboards in the kitchen and along the mantel, and we can decorate those if not today, then tomorrow. If you're available," she added quickly, suddenly aware of how easily she assumed he'd be around.

It wouldn't do to start thinking that way. At all.

But he replied, "Sure," without a hint of anything untoward in his tone. "Later, I'd like to go up to Trail's End and look in on the husky we operated on, just to make sure he's doing okay."

the bustle of it, and never knowing what will come in next."

"You have the mind and temperament for it, I suspect."

Surprised, she asked, "What do you mean?"

He shrugged. "Not everyone can keep cool under stress, or be open to all possibilities, which you have to when you're trying to diagnose patients. From what I've seen today, those are both qualities you possess in spades. They must have served you well in SAR too."

"I guess," she replied, ridiculously flattered by his factual tone.

"Do you miss it? Search and rescue?"

"Sometimes," she replied honestly. Somehow it was easy to talk to him out here in the open, the cold prickling her face, the smell of pine in the air. "The comradery, and the act of helping people under tricky situations. But there are parts I'd rather forget, and unfortunately, those are the ones that stick with me."

He tossed the branches he'd just cut onto the sled and turned to her, their gazes meeting, snagging.

"What parts?"

She wanted to turn away, refuse to tell him, but something inside was clamoring to tell the story, to try to leach some of the constant fear away.

Would he judge her as a coward, if he heard what had happened?

"Bax and I were on the slopes, looking for a skier who'd gone off the marked trails. There was an avalanche warning in effect, but the team can't think about that when they're trying to find someone."

She paused, took a deep breath, trying to slow her racing heart.

"We got caught in an avalanche, and buried. Bax was injured, but he still managed to dig me out."

"God, Elise." He took a step toward her and then stopped. "I'm sorry. You must have been terrified."

"I was, at the time, and even after a few months, I realized I still was. Even today I froze, coming through the tunnel, because I had a flashback when I heard the rumble of snow falling from the barn roof. There's no room for error or fear when you're on a rescue, and I knew I'd be a danger to the team, so I quit."

Those dark eyes of his surveyed her, seeming, as they so often did, to be looking into the heart of her.

"Do you want to go back to it?"

"I don't know," she said, shaken to honesty by his question. "Sometimes I do, and then I know I'm too scared to risk it. Yet it feels like I gave up on something I was so proud and happy to do, and that's almost worse than the fear."

He frowned, his brows coming together for an instant. "You're going to have to decide what's more important, I think—the fear or the determination to get past it. But you're the only one who can make that choice."

"You're right, but it's not a choice I feel strong enough to make right now."

He nodded before turning back to his chore. "Give yourself some time."

At his words, something eased inside, as though she had just been waiting to hear that advice to be able to relax. And the pangs of guilt and loss she usually felt when talking about it were softer, somehow more bearable.

When she decided they had enough boughs, and they were heading back to the house, she worked up the courage to ask a question that had been nagging at her all day.

"Is your father still alive?"

"He is, but he has advanced dementia."

"I'm sorry."

He shrugged. "He's had it for a number of years, and it progressed slowly at first. Then he had a series of strokes, and all at once, his condition deteriorated rapidly. He's nonverbal and barely ambulatory now."

"I'm sorry," she said again, knowing how inadequate the words were, but unable to find any better.

Rohan slanted her a look. "That's kind of you to say, considering what he put you through."

"Whatever he did, whatever his reasons, that's no way to end your days."

"I know."

There was something in his tone—sadness and anger all mixed together into the type of pain she knew all too well—that brought her to a halt and made her wish she could alleviate it in some small way.

"Do you want to see something totally ridiculous?" she asked, as he stopped walking, too, to turn a questioning gaze her way.

"Sure."

Elise bent to pick up some snow, saying, "For a dog as smart as Bax is, he completely loses his marbles around a snowball."

Even as she spoke, Bax noticed what she was doing, and came running, barking his head off. As he got closer, he screeched to a halt, then started jumping and prancing in a frenzy of delight.

"Bax, catch!"

Elise threw the snowball, and Baxter leaped to intercept it, biting at it in midair. The loosely packed ball disintegrated, of course, but after it

did, the dog looked shocked and began a con-
centrated hunt for it. As he turned in circles,
snuffling on the ground, Elise prepared another
ball.

"Bax, look."

His comical expression of surprise on seeing what he obviously thought was the same
ball, magically back in her hand, never failed to
amuse her. And she was happy to hear Rohan
snort with laughter, too.

"He looks that way every time," she said,
throwing the next snowball. "As though I've
tricked him, and he can't figure out how."

When Baxter reacted the same way the second time, Rohan's amusement turned to actual
laughter. Encouraged by the sound, and the joy
on his face, Elise threw the next ball at him instead of for Bax. The situation quickly devolved
into an out-and-out snowball fight between
them, with Baxter jumping about, barking and
capering.

It was a much-needed moment of levity, and
they were still laughing as they finally pulled
the sled into the garage.

Yet, despite her laughter, Elise almost wished
she hadn't seen this side of Rohan again. One
that was so redolent of his younger self it made
her yearn, wanting something that no longer
existed.

* * *

Even with the laughter, Rohan couldn't shake the disquiet he'd felt as he spoke about his father. There were so many unanswered questions regarding their relationship, and about why the older man had done the things he had in life. Rohan had always intended, at some point, to sit down with his father, perhaps over a glass of rum, and talk about their shared past. Ask all the questions he'd known his father wouldn't have answered in Rohan's youth, in the hopes they could talk as men rather than as parent and child.

Of course, now it would never happen, and with the kind of role model his father had been, Rohan couldn't help wondering what kind of father *he*'d be.

The fear that he wouldn't know how to relate to his son, that he'd mess up somehow, was nagging at him, eating away at his insides.

They hung garlands of boughs in the living room and festooned them with lights, to the accompaniment of Titan's running commentary. Then, while he arranged more boughs above the kitchen cupboards, Elise noted, "You're very quiet."

He stepped down from the ladder and stood back to view his handwork. "Just wondering how Jeevan and I will get along."

He tried to keep his voice light, but he didn't think she was fooled, since she put her hand on his arm and looked at him with compassion shining in her eyes.

"I think you'll get along fine. Yes, you're his parent, but it won't be like meeting him as a child. You're both adults, and both fine men. It might take a little time to find common ground, because of the situation, but I think you'll find it."

"Do you have an adult relationship with him?"

Her smile was soft, a little rueful.

"It's hard for me right now, because it was always him and me, and I was always the one in control. Once he went off to university, I had to start stepping back from my role as parent and give him the room to become whatever he wanted to be."

She sighed and glanced away. "Everyone seems to think there's some particular point in life when parents stop treating their kids as children and accept them as adults, but it's not as clear-cut as that. He'll always be my baby, but now I have to walk a fine line on a slippery slope, so he doesn't think I'm interfering in his life too much."

"I don't have the best experience on how fathers and sons relate to each other," he told her, knowing he had to be as honest as he could be, if he hoped for her help. "And I've become less and less social over the years, so my interpersonal skills are rusty, at best. I just want to do the right thing by him, and I'm not sure I know how."

There were so many other things he worried about, including the aftereffects of that long-ago accident, which seemed set to stay with him forever.

Although he'd retained most of his memory, was able to recall all he'd learned in school, knew his family and friends, something else had happened to his brain as a result of the crash. Something above and beyond the loss of those crucial seven months.

He couldn't remember having emotions about anything prior to awaking in the hospital. Couldn't recall how he'd felt during important times of his life.

In a way, he couldn't remember what it meant to be loved, and on the whole, accessing emotion had remained difficult.

Oh, he'd felt things—anger, sorrow when his mother died—but always at a distance, as though the hole in his memory banks had created a barrier between him and the world.

She squeezed his arm, her expression one of understanding.

"It's an unthinkable situation you've found yourself in, and it'll take time to figure it all out. Be kind to yourself. I'm sure everything will be fine."

Her assurance was generous, but was she comparing him to the young man he once was? The one who no longer existed?

The sensation that washed through him was familiar.

It was the urge to escape—an instinct to flee that came over him any time talk of his younger days surfaced. That urge to turn away, both from the conversations and the people wanting to have them, had led him into a solitary life.

Yet he couldn't do it now. Not when it meant forgoing a chance to meet his child.

And to spend a bit more time with the woman who'd given him this unexpected, glorious gift.

Again, honesty propelled him to say, "I'm not the man you knew, twenty-seven years ago. I've changed and—according to some—not for the better."

Her eyebrows rose, and her gaze searched his. Then the corners of her lips tilted up.

"If you were, after all this time, I'd say you suffered from a severe case of arrested development. Everyone changes, as life goes on, but I can say that the best qualities you had when I knew you are still very much in evidence. If they weren't, I'd probably not have said anything to you about Jeevan."

Her forthright words and acceptance made something warm bloom in his chest and spread its heat out through every vein in his body. He didn't know what the sensation was—could put no name to it—but perhaps a shadow of it crossed his face, for her eyes widened.

Once more he couldn't help noticing the sweet curve of her mouth, the way it softened, and the tip of her tongue briefly peeked out to touch her lower lip.

He wanted to kiss her, pull her into his arms, but fought the impulse.

"Nothing good can come of this." He hadn't planned to say the words aloud, but they echoed between them, and Elise nodded slowly.

"You're right, of course," she whispered, but Rohan realized their lips were closer together than they'd been before. So close he felt the rush of her breath, warm against his mouth.

Had he moved? Or had she?

Did it really matter, when his hands had already found her waist, and hers gripped his forearms?

"Elise." He'd planned to say more: *We can't. Tell me to stop.* Anything, in a last-ditch attempt to stem the tide of desire trying to drag him under. But his voice caught in his throat, and her name came out more like a plea.

The muted chime of a phone sounded from the table behind them, and they both froze. Almost simultaneously they stepped back, and he saw a warm rush of color stain her cheeks before she could turn away.

Walking to the table, she picked up her phone.

"Jeevan is in Hong Kong. He's been bumped from his original flight but hopes to get on another soon."

Rohan let out a long, silent breath, battling to get his wayward libido under control.

The best thing he could do would be to get away, try to make sense of what was happening between them.

He cleared his throat.

"I'm going to run up to Trail's End and check on the husky."

That would give him a little time to himself to work out what to do.

Elise nodded, her gaze unclouded, seemingly clear of the doubts and worries—and the lust— swirling through him.

"I'm going to put on dinner so it'll be ready when you get back."

He nodded. "Sounds good. And after we've eaten, if you want, we can go do the shopping."

"Okay," she said, giving him a little smile before turning to open the fridge.

As he put on his coat and headed out the door, what struck him was how homey the conversation sounded. Almost domestic.

And how damned right.

CHAPTER NINE

ELISE COULDN'T BELIEVE she'd almost kissed Rohan, and each time she thought of it, tingles spread up her spine, and desire ran, warm and sultry, through her entire body. She couldn't even find solace in the mundane, like she usually did, and as she fixed dinner, her mind kept going back to those thrilling moments.

Her response to his closeness didn't surprise her. Not really. Rohan was as attractive to her as he'd been all those years before, and the day had been an emotional one, filled with revelations and drama.

She was also discovering much to like about the older Rohan. His calm and compassion, the way he listened to her, his full attention focused on her words and expression. More than once he'd caught her off guard with his insightful comments and questions.

But even more important, she liked how much thought he was obviously putting into meeting

Jeevan and what he could do to make their relationship a good one. His eagerness made her heart sing and boded well for the future.

What wouldn't bode well was the undercurrent of lust flowing between them.

It wasn't hard to tell he wanted to keep some distance between them, and she was quite sure doing anything about their attraction would be a bad thing in the long run.

Once the novelty of their reunion wore off, having slept together would make things uncomfortable.

She'd made a big pot of chicken stew the week before and frozen it in batches. Now she heated some up, planning to add dumplings once it was simmering. As she mixed the dough, her thoughts turned once more to Rohan, and her breath caught in her throat.

He'd looked so uncomfortable, almost shocked, at their near-kiss, but she'd also seen the desire shimmering in his eyes. It was a look she recognized, even after all these years, and it still had the same effect on her as it had before.

Turning the burner down to low, she decided to have a shower while Rohan was gone.

While Ben's rescue had happened just that morning, it felt as though days had passed since then, and somehow the thought of a warm shower to wash away the day was infinitely appealing.

Having enjoyed her shower, she checked the pot and then went to make up the bed in the spare room and put out towels for Rohan. Wondering if he still liked an extra blanket when he slept, she went and got one, laying it out, just in case.

It was weird to know so much about a man but still consider him something of a stranger. Yet that was exactly how this crazy situation felt.

They'd somehow found their way back together after almost thirty years, their story almost perfectly bookended by accidents—one that tore them apart, the other reuniting them.

But she reminded herself that it wasn't a reunion, really. More a reintroduction—happenstance that fortunately also gave back to her son the father he'd never known.

That was what was important.

Nothing else.

By the time she finished, it was time to add the dumplings to the stew. After putting some rolls in the oven, she set about making a salad. As she went to open the fridge, she caught sight of the picture of Jeevan she always kept on the door.

Love for her son overwhelmed her, brought

her to tears. She'd missed him so much. It had been a constant ache in her heart. At least when he was at university, she'd known he was in the same country, although miles away. While he was abroad, she'd fretted and worried every day. Now she wondered how he'd feel when he discovered his supposedly long-deceased father was actually still alive.

When he was growing up, she'd tried to gauge how he was dealing with not having his father around, but he'd always assured her he was fine. During his rebellious teenage years, she'd wondered if having a solid father figure, or even a male influence on a day-to-day basis, would have curbed some of his wilder impulses.

Jeevan had had his Uncle Ray, Elise's brother-in-law, while they lived in Calgary, but once they'd moved to Banff when Jeevan was fourteen, it had just been the two of them.

How would Rohan coming back into their lives, and hearing why he'd been absent, affect their son?

There was no way to know until Jeevan got home and found out, but Elise couldn't help worrying anyway.

As she was cutting up cucumbers, her phone rang. It was Rohan.

"Everything okay?" she asked, wondering if

he'd changed his mind about staying there after their near-kiss.

"Yes, but I wanted you to know I'll be a little longer."

"The husky isn't doing well?"

"The one we operated on is fine, but the female has been acting up since the barn collapse. Nathan thought she was missing the male, and took her in to see him briefly earlier, but it didn't help. She only settled down when I went and took her out of the kennel, and I thought I'd just stay with her a while and see if I can calm her down enough to not have her howling all night."

"Bring her back here," Elise said. "Maybe having Bax for company will help."

There was a short silence, and she wished she could see his face, to perhaps get a hint of what he was thinking.

"She isn't house-trained, Elise."

"Bring some pee pads with you, and we'll keep her and Bax sequestered in the kitchen overnight. I'm not some shrinking violet who'll get upset over a bit of a mess in the morning."

The sound he made was something between a snort and a chuckle.

"Are you sure?"

"Definitely."

"Well, then, I'll see you in a few minutes."

"And for goodness' sake, give her a name. We can't expect her to listen to us if she doesn't know we're talking to her."

He laughed then, before hanging up, and the sound turned her insides to molten desire, and her legs to jelly.

What was it about that laugh that affected her this way? And had her thinking the kinds of thoughts she'd firmly told herself she shouldn't have?

Like if making love with him would be as magical and fulfilling as it had been when they were young. He'd instinctively known where to touch her, how to seek out her pleasure zones and, after taking her to the edge of orgasm, bring her to completion. Just thinking about it made nerve endings she'd almost forgotten she had roar back to life, and pushed tingling heat to all her erogenous zones.

During those heady months, they'd spent hours exploring their sexuality together. Neither of them had been virgins, but he'd often said he'd never had the type of satisfaction he'd found with her, and she'd readily admitted it was the same for her. Just kissing him had been an exercise in pleasure back then. One of her favorite memories was of them sitting on a bluff in Algonquin Park, surrounded by glorious autumn colors, kissing and kissing, and stopping only when they heard others coming up the trail.

That was where the picture of Rohan in her living room was taken, when she'd caught him in a moment of joy and impulsively snapped the shot. It showed, she thought, the essence of the man she'd fallen for so hard.

But he remembered none of that—and in a way she was glad. While he worried that she may be judging him against the person he was then, she didn't have to consider how he would view the changes in her—both physical and emotional—in return.

The young woman who'd luxuriated in delicious, rebellious passion no longer existed. In her place had grown a woman who'd learned to be steady, calm, controlled.

That was the woman she now needed to depend on, to put aside her erotic, potentially destructive impulses and keep him at arm's length.

With that pep talk, she went back to fixing the salad, but the heat that had flooded her stubbornly refused to abate, and her heart gave a little stutter when she heard his vehicle arrive.

The husky took some coaxing to get inside, and it was Baxter who seemed to have convinced her eventually, but once she came in, she swiftly settled down, sharing a bed with the golden.

"See, I told you Bax would help." Elise couldn't keep a hint of smugness from invading her tone as she put their dinner on the table. "Have you decided on a name for her yet?"

"Yes, you told me, and no, I haven't given her a name. We usually wait for either the fosterer or adopters to do that."

He pulled out her chair for her, waiting until she was seated to sit down.

"Well, I think that's silly. She needs rehabilitation, which also means learning her manners and basic commands, as well as socialization. I don't see how that's possible if she doesn't have a name to respond to. I'm going to call her Phoebe."

He just smiled and, picking up his spoon, said, "This smells delicious."

She knew a change of subject when she heard one, so she started on her salad. Swallowing the first bite, she said, "Chicken and dumplings is one of Jeevan's favorites. I was telling myself off for cooking as much of it as I did a couple days ago and was resigned to eating it for weeks. But since he's coming home, I won't have to worry."

He glanced up, his eyes gleaming. "Maybe you had a premonition that he would be here for Christmas after all?"

"Nope." She shook her head as she reached

for a roll. "I was absolutely sure he wouldn't be. He was so excited to see Australia—all those birds." She chuckled. "I asked him whether he'd go to the Great Barrier Reef, or travel to Sydney to see the Opera House or Bondi Beach, but he said probably not. His friend had some bush treks arranged so they could go bird-watching."

"I think I'll have to have words with him. I've heard the bird-watching on Bondi Beach is pretty amazing."

"Ooh…" Elise gave his deadpan expression a narrow-eyed glare, even though she saw the devilish humor in his gaze. "Don't you become a bad influence."

"What?" He tried for an innocent look and failed. "He likes birds."

She swatted his hand before going back to her meal. "Watch yourself, buddy."

As he was eating, Rohan couldn't help watching Elise even while they joked around—the way she moved, the shape of her lips, the delicate yet strong hands.

No matter how he tried to force himself to stop, his gaze tracked back to her again and again, taking in all the nuances of her expression.

Just as they finished their meal, a huge yawn

took him by surprise, and she gave him a knowing look.

"It's been a long day. I think we can leave the shopping for tomorrow, don't you? Why don't you take a shower and go to bed?"

"It's too early for bed. If I turn in now, I'll be up at three in the morning, but I could use a shower. Besides, I want to see Jeevan's pictures."

"Sure. If you like."

The memory of her smile, as she agreed, followed him down the corridor to the room she directed him to.

She seemed so happy that he wanted to see the pictures. Didn't she realize how amazingly special that would be to him?

But how could she, really?

Jeevan had been a part of her life since he was born. An unbroken chain of love connected them in ways Rohan could hardly fathom. There was no way she could begin to understand how it felt for him, after all those lonely, somehow barren years, to be presented with the gift of the chance to know—to love—his child.

It was like being given a second chance, a new lease on life, and he was going to grab ahold of it with both hands.

Going to give it everything he had.

He felt a bit better after his shower and wandered back out to find her in the living room, a stack of photo albums beside her.

She'd turned on the lights in the garlands they'd put up that afternoon, and Rohan wondered what her Christmas tree would be like when decorated. Would it be filled with colorful, silly toys, remnants of Jeevan's childhood, or would it be elegant and color-coordinated? Somehow, he thought the former. She struck him as a woman of sentiment, behind that no-nonsense, strong exterior.

As he sat next to her on the couch, she said, "I got in the habit of putting albums together and kept doing it even when the digital revolution took over, although I have hundreds of other pictures on the computer."

She placed them on his lap and said, "The years they span are on the spines, and I think they're in order, but you can check." Straightening, she stretched. "I'm going to take the dogs out. If there's anything you want to know about, just ask."

"Thank you," he said, battling disappointment that she wasn't sticking around to look at the pictures with him.

Yet that same sense of excitement he'd felt earlier superseded discontent soon, as he opened the first album and found a record of Jeevan's birth, complete with foot and handprints.

That was when he knew he was in trouble—
that what he'd thought of as an interesting way
to learn a bit more about his son was going to be
an emotionally devastating event. The knowledge almost made him close the album and walk
away, but he fought the impulse.

All this time he'd thought he'd lost the ability
to feel emotion, but maybe he'd just been too
frightened to feel. Too hurt to want to. Looking
at the pictures would hurt, but perhaps also, in
some way, heal.

So he forced himself to focus, to accept the
pain of loss.

Those tiny hands and feet that he'd never got
to see. Toes he'd never got to kiss. Palms he'd
never got to wash.

He wanted to go back, to experience it all.
To be there for the middle-of-the-night feed-
ings. For rocking baby Jeevan to sleep. Even
for diaper duty.

Elise had had to do it all herself, taking on the
full responsibility of motherhood without him,
and the knowledge tore into him like a lance
through the heart.

For a long time he couldn't move, except to
run his finger over the inked lines until, eventually, he forced himself to turn the page.

Elise, younger, disheveled and pale, and a
wrinkly, obviously just-born Jeevan lying on

her breast, his face turned away from the camera. He had a full head of dark hair, and Rohan lifted his hand to touch his nape, just where his hair swirled. The spot every barber complained about, because it was impossible to cut it so the strands lay flat.

"Who has a cowlick at the back of their head?" one had complained.

Rohan did. And so did his son.

What else did they share? The shape of their toes or fingers? Perhaps an affinity for sweets, or seafood?

He wanted to know, even as each revelation, every discovery, would tear at his heart.

With a deep breath, he turned another page, trying to hold it together, taking his time to view the photos, noting the subtle changes as Jeevan grew. One thing never wavered, though, and that was the love clearly visible in Elise's eyes whenever she was looking at their child. There were other people in some of the pictures, but Rohan hardly spared them a glance. The only people he was interested in were his son and the woman who'd given him life.

"How're things going?"

Lost in the moment, in the pain, he hadn't heard her coming back, and looked up. She was a blur, and he blinked to clear his vision. And it was then he realized he'd teared up, looking at this record of all he'd missed.

All he'd lost.

"Oh, Rohan. Don't."

And then she was there, holding him, and he could let go, somehow sure she wouldn't let him fall.

CHAPTER TEN

"IT'S OKAY. IT'S OKAY."

Elise didn't know what else to say to the man trembling in her arms, or how to comfort him. She thought he was crying, but he did so without sound, just the silent, quaking body expressing sorrow and regret.

Because she knew there was no real comfort she could offer.

What he was seeing, what it appeared he mourned, was the past, and the lost chance to be a part of all that was laid out two-dimensionally before him in the albums. To experience what was pictured in real time, as she had.

She remembered the feel of holding Jeevan as a newborn, a baby, a toddler. Remembered the weight of him, the scent, as he went from baby powder sweetness to grubby little boy, to the teenager who wouldn't leave the house without the stinky cologne he favored at the time.

There'd been fights over clothes, about how

he wore his pants, and the ugly hat he'd found on sale somewhere and wore until it started to unravel. Strong words exchanged over report cards and inappropriate friends, rumors of him sneaking cigarettes—which he thankfully didn't become addicted to—and the snake she once found in his room.

Elise knew she wouldn't change any of it, although there were parts she would prefer not to relive.

Rohan, she now realized, would give anything to have been there for all of it, and was grieving the inability to do so.

So there really were no words to ease his anguish, or to make it right. All she could do was hang on and try to see him through.

In a way, she'd been where he was, just in a different way.

She was eternally thankful for her sister, Emma, who'd taken her in and held her while she wept for Rohan. Emma had traveled the road of loss with her, encouraging her to think of the future, not just of the past. Perhaps Elise could do the same for Rohan now.

"You can't go back in time, Rohan, but you have a lot to look forward to. I know it hurts to know what you missed, but there's time to start over, to build a relationship with Jeevan, and be happy."

He lifted his head from her shoulder. His eyes were red, and the long, dark lashes damp, and her heart ached for him even more.

This close she could clearly see the fine lines of his scars, noticed for the first time how close to his eye one of them went. Without thought she touched it, thankful the laceration had stopped short, and he hadn't been blinded.

"Were we in love, Elise—back then?"

The truth was hard to admit, but it was the only way to help him move forward.

"Yes, we were. Very much, although I held back as much as I could, too frightened to give in to it completely. You wanted us to make a life together, and we were to discuss how we would move forward after you came back. You said you'd wait and see where I would be doing my residency before looking for a job, because you wanted me to go wherever I wanted, rather than follow you."

His gaze searched hers, and she held it effortlessly, needing him to see she was willing to tell him whatever he wanted to know.

"Was Jeevan planned?" He hesitated a beat, then continued, "I mean, we're both doctors. It's not as though we didn't know where babies come from."

That made her smile, just a little, as she shook her head. "Not planned, but not avoided, either.

We were in Algonquin Park, and one of our bags fell out of the canoe and got swept away. My birth control pills were in it, and we both knew the possible consequences but didn't take any other precautions."

It had been, she'd realized long after, the beginning of capitulation on her part, the start of admitting how much she loved him. But she hadn't gotten the chance to tell him, and that, as much as anything else, had intensified her grief.

His gaze turned inward for a moment, then it sharpened back on her, his expression one of regret—sadness.

"I wish I could remember it all. I wish I had been there for you, and for Jeevan. Knowing I can't go back doesn't lessen the regret and the guilt."

"I know." Unable to tame the impulse to touch him, she pressed her palm to his cheek, as she had so many times all those years ago, the nostalgia of it almost too much to bear. "But neither of those will help you now. Look to the future, rather than pining for a past that's long gone."

As if by instinct, he twined his fingers around hers and turned his head to kiss the inside of her wrist. Elise's breath caught in her throat at the tender sensation, so achingly familiar.

When he looked back at her, his eyes were even darker, slumberous, as if he, too, recognized the connection to the past, although she knew he didn't.

Never could.

But before that thought could take root and cause her to pull away, he leaned closer and laid his lips on hers. There was no attempt at mastery or coercion, both of which would have caused her to resist.

Instead, it was a gentle salute, a question and a subtle seduction, all in one. His mouth was firm and warm and intensely exciting, drawing out within her all her desire, the longing she'd been wrestling with all day. And as his lips moved softly over hers, it was like slipping into one of the dreams she still had about him, where they laughed and loved, expressing the passion that had burned so bright between them.

The need to be with him, even just one more time, was too strong to resist. So, instead of drawing away, she looped her arms around his neck and drew him in closer, deepening the kiss.

She wasn't sure how Rohan would react. He had no way of knowing, as she did, how much pleasure they had found in each other before, the perfect way they melded, the satisfaction they could achieve. It wouldn't have surprised her if he had set her aside, think it a step too far.

But he didn't.

And anticipation turned to bliss as he returned her embrace and took over.

Just a kiss. One kiss more, and then I'll stop.

But those were lies he told himself, because he didn't want to stop.

Ever.

And Rohan kept kissing Elise, sinking deeper and deeper in the rushing passion swirling around them.

Sweet. She tasted sweet, the flavor unlike any he'd encountered before, but more intoxicating than twelve-year-old rum.

The sensation of her body against his was almost too sublime to be real.

They fit together perfectly, aligning as though made just for this purpose.

For each other.

For loving.

He shifted, distantly aware of the albums sliding off his lap onto the floor, and urged her to straddle his thighs. Without hesitation she nimbly complied, and he groaned into her mouth as she settled over him. Her nipples pressed into his chest, even through the layers of their clothing, and the crux of her thighs against his erection generated mind-blowing friction.

And still they kissed, mouths slipping against each other, tongues tangling together.

He didn't know how far she wanted to go, or when she'd tell him to stop. All he knew was he would make love to her as much, and for as long, as she'd let him.

When he slid his lips along the line of her jaw, she tipped her head back, offering the long line of her throat, and he didn't hesitate to comply with her silent request. At the first touch of his mouth on her neck she moaned, low and sweet, and shivered, the sensation of her pleasure traveling through her and into his hands.

His fingers moved restlessly against her back, wanting to dip under her clothes, but he was unwilling to take the chance to do anything to make her retreat. With his pulse racing, breath sawing in and out of his chest, he kept nibbling, licking and sucking at her throat, reveling in the passionate sounds she made and the way her hands clutched at his arms.

Elise leaned back so suddenly he was taken by surprise, and his heart missed a beat as he feared she'd had enough. Then she reached down and grasped the hem of her sweater and pulled it off over her head.

Transfixed, Rohan stared at the bounty of her breasts, clad only in a lacy bra, peachy nipples clearly visible under the sheer fabric. His hand trembled as he used his index finger to trace along the curved edge of the cup, and she gasped softly, goose bumps breaking out across her chest and arms. When he dipped beneath the lace and touched one puckered areola, she shivered again, and a rush of color stained her skin, rising up into her throat.

Entranced, Rohan slid his hand across to the other side, repeating the teasing caress. The contrast of his darker skin against her lighter one was sublime, as was the softness of her flesh beneath his finger. Heat rose along his spine and filled his belly as the desire between them flared even hotter.

He was taken by surprise when she reached back and undid her bra, sliding it down her arms so she sat before him bare to her waist.

He wanted to tell her how beautiful she was, how he ached for her, but his voice had deserted him, unable to function in the storm his need created within.

Her hips moved against him, making him groan her name, and when she cupped her breasts, offering them to him, and he bent to take one nipple between his lips, he knew himself lost.

And somewhere at the back of his mind, he hoped never to be found again, if it meant returning to the bleak existence he'd been living just the day before.

There was no way to measure how long he

spent lavishing attention on her sensitive flesh. It could have been hours, or minutes. He didn't care. Time had no meaning. All that was important was the way she trembled and moaned, her hands on the back of his head, holding him there.

But then she lifted his head so as to kiss him again, and again, pulling up the back of his shirt, obviously wanting no more barriers between them.

As she broke the kiss to remove it, a cold finger of fear trickled down his spine.

His body wasn't as it had been all those years ago, when she'd first known him. Now it was scarred, pitted with the evidence of the accident and the operations needed to put him back together.

It had never mattered to him before, but now embarrassment made him want to cover himself, so she, who had known him whole, wouldn't see what he'd become.

"Elise…"

But it was too late. Her darkened gaze wandered over his body, and her fingers trailed across his belly, chest and shoulders, seeking and caressing each raised ridge, mark and scar. Just as she had touched his face, tracing the passage of his physical injuries, as though reading them like braille.

When her eyes met his, she must have seen his shame and fear, because her lips, so full and lush from his kisses, lifted into a gentle smile.

"You're still beautiful," she said softly. "And I want you."

Then she slid off his lap to stand in front of him, holding out her hands.

There was a dreamlike quality to the moment, which had him putting all caution aside and standing to take her outstretched hands. Turning, she led him down the corridor and into a dimly lit bedroom, which smelled like her.

Far in the back of his mind were all the worries, the questions arising from what they were doing.

Was she just lost in nostalgia, forgetting the present? Would she compare him to what he used to be, and find him wanting? Or regret this impulsive, passionate encounter? Tomorrow, would she want him gone, because they'd given in to lust instead of being sensible and thinking only of their son and his reactions?

Rohan tried to find the right words to ask all those questions, to find out if she was sure about what they were doing, but Elise turned to pull him close, and everything fled his mind.

Except her.

CHAPTER ELEVEN

DEEP INSIDE, ELISE knew she shouldn't allow herself to fall into fantasy, but it was impossible not to accept and welcome the surreal quality of once more loving Rohan.

She had never tried to forget him over the years, feeling that to do so would be a betrayal of all they'd shared, an insult to him and their son. There had been times when she'd believed it would be best to let his memory fade, like the old photographs in their album, but she could never quite achieve it.

And at night sometimes he came to her in her dreams. Then she would awaken with a familiar ache around her heart, and physical frustration as her companion for the rest of the day.

Even now her head stumbled over the thought of him being alive and in her arms, and she found it simpler to believe it a lucid, arousing figment of her imagination. Not even the sight of his scars brought her back to her senses. Instead, they filled her with tenderness, and gratitude for his survival.

It made it easier to be bold, demanding. To tell and show him what she wanted, and to revel in the perfection of his response and attentions.

Easier, too, to put aside questions and doubts.

This moment might never arise again, and Elise refused to let it pass without making the absolute best of it.

She turned on the lamp beside the bed, wanting to see him, as well as touch. He stood just inside the door, his expression dazed, but the dark fire in his eyes was thrillingly familiar and grew even hotter as she took off the rest of her clothes.

Then she lay on the bed and said, "Aren't you going to undress?"

He didn't reply and didn't take his eyes off her as he swiftly removed what he had on. When the last garment fell away, Elise held out her arms. Without hesitation he came to her, embracing her as though never to let go.

There. There. At last.

She pulled him in as tightly as she could, wrapping arms and legs around him, almost in tears at the feel of being skin to skin with him, as his scent inundated her head. Her heartbeat, already racing, quickened, and her body trembled as jagged shards of arousal fired through her system.

They kissed, and for Elise it was as though the intervening years hadn't existed, the sensations so familiar she was thrown back to the time when she was his love, and he was hers. And she allowed herself to forget the pain and heartbreak, concentrating only on the now and the echoes of then.

It may have been a long time, but she still knew how and where to touch him, the muscle memory intact. Running her fingers down the valley of his spine made him shiver, low sounds of pleasure flowing from his lips into her mouth. And as they shifted, twisting against each other, she found the spot, just beside his hip bone, and made him jerk in reaction.

Yet it was, in a sense, poking the bear, as his previously leisurely lovemaking morphed into a dedicated campaign to drive her wild.

He'd always been a deliberate lover, slow of hands, tender of touch, but now he seemed determined to stretch his caresses out until she lost control. She arched and stretched, mewls of delight and excitement breaking unfettered from her lips as he tasted and explored her, as though intent on learning her body's every secret.

He lingered for a long time over her stomach, his tongue tracing back and forth across her skin, the heat from his mouth making her bow up with the promise of what came next. Opening her eyes, she looked down and watched in rapt fascination, wanting to have a visual memory of the moment.

Then she realized what he was doing, and tears threatened. Beneath the tender, erotic trail were the stretch marks she'd been left with after giving birth to Jeevan.

As though sensing her regard, he lifted his gaze to hers, and in it she saw the same pleasure, desire and sense of loss she felt deep inside. It made the moment sweeter, hotter as his lips drifted lower...

Everything slowed for a moment, and at the first soft touch of his lips between her thighs, she cried out, her need suddenly building, her body tightening. His hold on her grew firmer, his sole focus seeming to take her to the brink of insanity and then ease her back, letting her catch her breath before beginning again.

She heard herself first pleading, then demanding, and then begging for completion. But when it came it was like a lightning strike, taking her by surprise, sending sharp currents of almost unbearable ecstasy over and through her, so she wept at the power.

Shifting up on the bed, he held her until the

* * *

Rohan listened to Elise's breathing deepen as he lay beside her, wide awake and wondering if her turning away was an omen of things to come.

It wouldn't surprise him if it was. He'd seen the struggle she'd gone through today, coming to terms with him being alive, accepting he was—no matter the capacity—back in her life once more.

Who could blame her if sleeping with him was just an impulse born of an emotionally shocking day?

Yet their lovemaking had been more beautiful and heartrending than any he'd experienced before. Holding her had felt right. Touching her had awakened in him instincts—of tenderness and caring—he'd long thought dead. And while it hadn't brought any memories to life, at the same time it was familiar, comfortable. His mind might not recognize her, but his body seemed to, and the intimacy of that had almost undone him.

Once more his thoughts turned to the loss he'd sustained, not of his memories, but of the time he could have shared with this beautiful and remarkable woman. And with his son. The anger at being cheated of a life he was sure would have been more fulfilling and satisfy-

final tremors of her orgasm ceased, then he lifted her chin to look deep into her eyes.

"Thank you," he said.

But before she could ask him for what, he was kissing her again, and the swift rise to desire began once more.

This time she wasn't letting him take the lead, and she set about arousing him as thoroughly as he had her. When they were young, he used to like her to take charge whenever she wanted, and it seemed that hadn't changed. He didn't stop her as she rolled him onto his back and began her own form of loving torture.

Finally, he twined his fingers into her hair and gave a gentle tug.

"If you don't stop, I'm going to lose control."

She heard it in his tone, his accent thickening, his already deep voice little more than a growl, and it made her smile. Working her way up his body, she planted kisses at random intervals, watching the goose bumps feather up over his skin, pleased with the effect.

She straddled his thighs, her gaze taking in the ruddy tone staining his cheeks, the tension evident in his posture. Both face and body were different—older, scarred, battered—yet he was still Rohan, her lover.

Her love.

In that moment she made the choice to think

of him that way, even though she knew there would be adjustments to be made in the morning, realities to be faced.

It was simpler, since he didn't remember her and didn't have the same battles to fight. She was fine with that—glad of it—and tonight was just for her.

Not for Jeevan, or even for Rohan.

Just for her.

Her last chance to feel young again, and in love. To feel as though the rest of her life stretched before her, too long to contemplate the ending. The way she'd felt the last time they'd been together and hadn't ever since.

She shifted over him, took him deep, gasping at the sublime sensation, lost in the passion and the love flowing in her veins. Lost, perhaps, just a little in the past, too, although she kept her eyes open so she could watch his face tighten, his eyelids droop, as he surrendered to her lovemaking.

Rohan held her hips, helping her rise and fall, letting her set the pace. This time she felt it coming, the orgasm teasing her as it built, making her frantic.

"Elise…"

She knew the sound of her name, said just that way, was a warning. Rohan was close, trying to hold off, for her sake.

He reached between her thighs, his thumb seeking, finding her clitoris, and with a touch, he sent her skyrocketing, and immediately soared with her.

She pitched forward, boneless, onto his chest, and he caught her in his arms. Rolling to one side, he struggled with the sheet and comforter, finally getting it out from under their bums so he could pull it up to cover them.

Neither spoke, and he turned off the light, leaving them in the shifting shadows of moonlight on snow coming in through the drapes. It was a companionable silence, and in it Elise came to peace with what had happened. No regrets. Although it had been mind-blowing, it had also been a one-off.

Being the only one mired in the memories of the love they'd shared, she had no urge to make Rohan feel sorry for her, or as though his relationship with Jeevan was dependent on them being together.

No. Tonight really had been just for her—sentiment, and for pleasure. For one more sw memory to savor.

But as she dozed off, sadness crept close she turned away from the warmth of R ar arms, as though not to get used to the c ar she found in them.

ing than the one he'd been living bubbled once more to the surface.

Yet what good could come from yearning for the impossible? He had to accept the night, her lovemaking, as another gift, one he probably wouldn't be given again.

That was a good thing, on the balance. Establishing a relationship with her outside of the parental one left him vulnerable to the kind of pain he never wanted to feel again.

The agony of being a disappointment, of not being the man she thought or hoped he was.

Restless, his anxiety rising, he quietly slipped from the bed and the room, grabbing his pants as he went.

Putting back on the rest of his clothes, he went into the kitchen, stepping over the temporary barrier they'd set up to keep the husky from having free rein of the house. Both dogs looked up at the sound of his entrance, and when he went toward the door, got up to follow him.

Pausing to put on his coat and slip his feet into his boots by the back door, he contemplated whether the husky needed a leash, but decided it would be okay to let her run free. None of the rescue dogs had much experience with wide-open spaces and tended to stick close to what they considered safe territory. Of course, she'd only been here for a few hours, but with the way she closely shadowed Bax, Rohan thought she wouldn't stray far.

The cold air stung his cheeks, and he wrapped his scarf tighter around his neck, aware of the fact he wasn't as warmly dressed as he should be, but the need to be outside was almost primal. Something about the winter night spoke to his soul and eased his anxiety.

While his body continued to hum with pleasure, his mind swung in dizzying circles, thinking about Elise, Jeevan, the past, the future.

He knew without a doubt that there was no future between him and Elise. There would be no encore to the lovemaking. He couldn't afford to open himself up that way. Not when his relationship with Jeevan might be affected.

At one point in the past he'd thought about being a father, yet had never been sure he'd be any good at it. The aftermath of his accident, the way everyone criticized who he'd become, had made him believe himself unworthy of being a parent.

How do you love, when you can't seem to feel anything too deeply?

Yet, with the revelations of the day, that theory had been blown out of the water.

He was nothing but a mass of emotion right now, and the thought of meeting his son brought equal parts fear and pleasure crashing over him.

The knowledge of all he'd already lost in life was a constant refrain in his head, and he couldn't risk putting himself in a position to lose even more.

His sole focus had to be Jeevan, and making sure the lessons Rohan had learned from his own father showed him what *not* to do, so he could be, at the very least, a decent one.

And being that kind of man didn't include causing pain or disappointment to the child's mother.

Recalling how his father had become increasingly overbearing as time passed, while his mother faded to a kind of quiet shadow in the glare of her husband's bullying, made his stomach clench in disgust. He knew he wasn't like that, but there were myriad ways to hurt and to harm those closest to you.

Then he shook his head, trying to think of the future instead of the past.

Elise deserved better than him—as a lover, or more—but for Jeevan he'd have to find a way to be the best he could be, as a man, so as not to destroy his only chance of a good relationship with his son.

Calling for the dogs, he let them back inside and, after taking off his outerwear, went back into the living room. He picked up the albums again, losing himself in the pictures.

CHAPTER TWELVE

ELISE AWOKE EARLY on the day before Christmas Eve, her mind too sluggish and slow to bring up the list of her daily chores the way it usually did.

She knew she should get up—there was so much to do—but lay still for a moment more, wondering why everything felt so strange. Slightly askew.

Then it came to her.

She'd had another dream about Rohan making love with her, but this time, instead of feeling bereft and frustrated, she felt happy. Satiated.

Absolutely wonderful.

Then her heart started racing, as she remembered it hadn't been a dream. Rohan was not only alive but here in Banff, and her bed.

Or he had been in her bed.

A quick glance told her he was no longer there, and a rush of disappointment made her sigh.

When had he left? Stretching out her hand,

she found the sheets were cold, so she knew he'd been gone for at least a while.

Had he slept beside her? She wished she knew.

Then she forced herself to come back down to earth and leave the fantasyland she was tempted to remain in.

It didn't matter whether he'd slept there or not. In fact, them making love didn't matter, either, regardless of how magical and special it had been.

She'd recognized how selfish she was being, even while reveling in his touch, and now it was time to let her common sense and parental duty take precedence.

In the cold light of morning, the only matter of importance was breaking the news to Jeevan and giving him and Rohan a chance to develop a good relationship. Well, realistically, any kind of relationship would be a start, but it was up to her to step back—from them both—to give them the leeway to bond.

Elise wasn't naive enough to think it would be easy or happen in a flash. There'd already been one Christmas miracle; no need to be greedy and hope for another.

And there was the rest of her Christmas preparations to consider, she thought, swinging her legs out of bed with a decisive move. As she rose to her feet, she was determined that nothing would change, or be missed, of their traditional festivities, except that Rohan would be there, too.

But that realization had her suddenly plunking back down onto the bed, almost light-headed.

All those years ago, he'd promised to be back for Christmas, and hadn't come. That first year, heartbroken, she'd locked herself away from everyone but her sister and family, unable to bear the thought of Rohan no longer being with her, or able to return.

Then Jeevan had been born, and he'd filled some of the holes left in her heart. Given her a reason to go on.

But Christmas had never been the same.

She'd forced herself to celebrate every year, to give Jeevan the kind of Christmases children dream of, but her heart was never truly in it. Not for herself anyway. Oh, she'd enjoyed them through her son's eyes. His childish wonder had buoyed her spirits, and his laughter salved her wounded soul.

As he'd gotten older, he'd come to expect their holidays together to be mostly the same, and she'd complied, because by then it was tradition. Once they'd gone on a Caribbean cruise, her gift to him when he graduated with his first degree, but they'd agreed that while it was fun, it wasn't really Christmas. Home was where they preferred to be.

After all, she was his family—all there was locally, since Emma, her husband and kids had moved to British Columbia—and he was hers.

Now, after all this time, Rohan had showed up, and Elise had to accept nothing would ever be the same.

Part of her almost wished he'd been to blame for his desertion, so she could flippantly think, *Twenty-seven years late and a dollar short*. But he hadn't been, and for him, finding out he'd had a son whose existence had been kept from him was painful. She'd seen it in his eyes, in his expression, when he was looking at the photographs, and she'd known she wouldn't do anything to hurt him more.

Like give Jeevan a reason not to like him. And Jeevan, being very protective of his mother, would definitely have something to say if he thought they'd slept together and Rohan wasn't serious about the relationship.

And why would Rohan be inclined to be serious?

Sure, their sexual chemistry clearly was still off the charts, but he didn't *care* about her the way she cared about him. Not when he couldn't even remember her—when he couldn't remember the love they had so passionately shared.

Because it had never been just sex between them, all those years ago. Instead, there'd been an instant, mutual connection of their hearts and souls, although it had taken losing him for her to admit it. Having lost so much already in her life, she'd been loath to trust in the longevity of their relationship, and it had taken having Jeevan to prove she could never really love too much.

No matter the potential cost.

Elise remembered what Rohan and she had shared. Too bloody well, really. But there was no way she was going into a new relationship with him, knowing she was the only one capable of having that depth and strength of love rekindled.

Best to keep it friendly and light, and to forget about her romp down memory lane, even if the night together was best described as incendiary, and the chemistry between them combustible.

Decision made, she got up again and set to making the bed, trying to ignore how her stomach flipped and heart raced as Rohan's scent rose from her sheets.

While in the bathroom, she looked out of the window, and in the early morning light saw Rohan walking along the driveway, Baxter and

Phoebe following him. For a moment she allowed herself the luxury of watching and remembering the erotic, ecstatic night just gone.

The way he touched her had lit a fire within, and even now, despite knowing it shouldn't be repeated, she felt it smoldering beneath her skin.

Phoebe, who'd been slinking along behind Bax, suddenly paused, head cocked. Baxter stopped, too. The two dogs trotted over to the edge of the driveway, and then jumped over the snowbank to inspect something on the other side.

As Elise reached for her toothbrush, she noticed Rohan look back and realize the dogs weren't following. Of course he strode over to see what had them so interested and, once on the other side of the mound of snow, he stooped down.

What were they all looking at?

Hurrying through her morning routine, Elise pulled on a cozy sweater and pair of jeans and was on her way to the kitchen when she heard the back door open.

"Elise, can you come here a moment, please?"

"I'm here," she replied as she stepped through the door to find him cradling something in his hands. "What is that?"

"A raven. The dogs found it. It's still alive, but just barely."

Drawing closer, she saw the pitiful mound of black feathers cupped in his palm, and all her recent worries faded into the background.

"What do you need?" she asked, even as she was crossing to the utility cupboard to pull out a clean towel. "I have a hot-water bottle we can put it on."

He glanced at her with eyebrows raised. "I see this isn't your first avian rescue."

She snorted, folding the towel. "Nowhere near the first. Jeevan had a knack for finding injured birds and bringing them home. And he has a soft spot for the Corvidae family."

"It looks to be a youngster, probably a yearling," Rohan said, putting the raven gently on the outstretched towel. "And the wing is injured. Where can I put it, so I can examine it better?"

"Use the kitchen table," she replied, already halfway to the hall closet, where the hot water bottle was stored. "I can disinfect it later. And I think we still have a small cage in the garage. I'll go look."

"Could you get my medical bag out of my car, too, while you're out there?" Rohan had pulled off his jacket and scarf and was rolling up his sleeves.

"Sure."

First, though, she filled the hot-water bottle, and as Rohan lifted the bird, put it between the folds of the towel. To her surprise, the bird was already exhibiting some signs of life, but it wasn't struggling or showing fear, which made her wonder just how badly it was injured. Ravens usually fought to be free and away from humans, even when hurt, but this one was terribly lethargic.

By the time she got back with the cage and bag, Rohan had the raven covered by a drape of the towel, and the bird's dark eyes flickered.

"The poor fellow has a coracoid injury, and he's very thin," Rohan told her as she set his bag next to him.

"Broken?"

"No. From the swelling, it seems to be muscle damage, and it's probably been hurt for a while. I'm going to apply a figure-eight bandage to keep the wing immobilized, but we'll need to get it to a wildlife rehabilitation center. Is there one here?"

"No, I'm afraid not. I think the closest one is in Cochrane, about an hour away."

"I'll take it there, then, once I get it bandaged," he replied. "Rehabbing a bird like this is a full-time job—one I'm not prepared to take on right now."

"Thankfully Jeevan learned that quickly, too," she said. "He'd go and volunteer at the rehab center but knew he didn't have the time to take on too many cases himself. He also realized that we weren't set up to rehab and release, and he's a huge proponent of that, although he's aware not every bird can fend for itself in the wild once injured."

Rohan cut a long length of vet tape, and Elise moved closer to hold the raven while he wrapped the wing against its body. Their fingers brushed, and a shiver fired along her spine, making her breath catch in her chest.

He glanced up and his eyes gleamed for an instant, as though he was remembering the night before, and then the shutters came down, leaving his expression bland and unconcerned.

"Hold it just here," he said, showing her what he needed, his voice cool.

It shouldn't hurt. After all, wasn't she just not long before telling herself it would be better that there was nothing physical between them? She'd even been going over in her head what she'd say to him so he knew there'd be no repeat of their lovemaking.

But his coldness did sting, although she refused to reveal that to him. She would be her usual self, no matter what, and just be glad if he took the onus off her by making the decision not to push for a closer relationship.

As he wrapped the bird's wing against its body, her stomach grumbled, probably annoyed at not even having had a cup of coffee yet, and the corner of Rohan's lips twitched.

"I'm going to make breakfast when we're finished here," she said. "Want some, before you head to Cochrane?"

"That would be great," he replied, his skilled hands making short work of immobilizing the raven's wing. "I'm not sure this little guy is going to survive, so it makes sense to watch him for a little while before making the drive."

They prepared the cage with a liner, and once the bird was ensconced, she washed her hands and poured herself a cup of coffee. Rohan was at the sink, and now that she had a chance to really look at him, she realized he looked tired. Drawn.

"Are you feeling okay?" She used her doctor voice, although it was very much the woman worried about him. But before he could answer, she held up her hand and said, "And don't give me a stock 'I'm okay… I'm fine,' answer either. You look like hell."

He shook his head, brows coming together for an instant. "I'm just tired. I was too keyed up to sleep last night, and spent a few hours going through the pictures."

Was he worried about what had happened between them? He'd been put through the wringer the day before, and she didn't like the idea that their sleeping together was adding to his stress. Although before she'd thought to not say anything unless he brought it up, now she decided it was better out in the open, so it could be resolved, once and for all.

"About last night," she began, making sure to keep her voice clinical. "I let old emotions and nostalgia get the better of me, and I knew, even when it was happening, that it wasn't a good idea. But we're not kids, so let's talk about it and make sure we're on the same page."

"Okay," he said, in a distant, noncommittal tone that set her teeth on edge.

Then he just looked at her, eyebrows raised, as though waiting for her to continue. Tamping down her annoyance and hurt, Elise took a breath and said, "I can't allow my baggage to jeopardize your chance to build a relationship with Jeevan. I know he's an adult, but I think he needs to see us as separate units at this point. We shouldn't muddy the waters by fooling around, making him think, even for a second, that we might get together."

He gave her a long look, while nodding slowly.

"Thank you for the candor, and I think you're right," he said, finally. "It wasn't a good idea."

She'd said it first, so why did his agreement

wound her so much? But they'd started down this road and needed to get to the end.

"I think the main things we need to concentrate on are how to tell Jeevan and how to be supportive of his reaction, whatever that may be."

"I agree. Our son has to be our first concern."

He looked away, and she noticed a muscle jumping in his jaw. Realizing he wasn't as calm as he appeared, she reached out without thought and touched his hand.

"It'll be fine. I'm sure of it."

"I'll keep hoping you're right," he replied, his voice cool, as he eased his hand free. "So what's on the agenda for you today?"

She followed his lead, turning to open the fridge, pretending casualness and a deep interest in picking out sausages and eggs. "As soon as I'm finished here, I have to run out to the supermarket, since I need baking supplies, as well as groceries. I'm planning to make all of Jeevan's favorite treats later this morning. Do you think the raven might want to eat? We could try it with an egg."

"Not right now," Rohan replied. "I don't think it's recovered enough for food just yet. And they'll have mealworms at the rescue, which might be better for it at this point."

He walked to the window and stood looking out, rubbing his cheek.

Then he turned back toward her and said, "While you're out shopping, I'll run the raven over to Cochrane, and then go up to Trail's End for a bit. I thought I'd give them a hand, since Janice has more than enough on her plate."

"Okay," she replied, thinking he sounded glad to be getting away. Almost relieved. "By the way, would you like to come to the SAR fund-raiser tomorrow night? It's usually a lot of fun. There are silent auctions, and the dinner is catered by a really great company. You could ask Tom about Phoebe then, too."

"What's the dress code? I didn't bring anything but jeans when I came up here."

There it was again, that flatness in his tone, as though he were simply being polite, and not totally engaged in the conversation.

"It's dressier than that. You'd definitely feel out of place in jeans. Most of the men wear suits, or sports coats at least."

He shrugged. "I'll buy something. It's been a while since I bought a new suit, and I know it won't go to waste."

"We can go into town later," she said as she turned on the stove. With everything else going on, she had yet to make out her shopping list. "I need to buy a few gifts."

He walked back to the cage and bent to look at the raven.

Without glancing at her, he said, "I was thinking… I want to get a gift for Jeevan, but I don't want him to think I'm trying to buy his affection, or anything like that. Will you give me some advice on what he might like?"

"Sure," she said lightly. Despite the hurt caused by his renewed coldness, her heart melted at the thought he was putting into how to treat his son. "We'll go out this evening and take a look around the shops. You can get your suit, too, then."

"Excellent," he said.

But although the conversation sounded normal, even friendly, she saw the way all expression had fallen from his face, and felt the distance between them widening.

And telling herself not to be stupid about it didn't ease the pain.

CHAPTER THIRTEEN

AFTER DROPPING THE raven off in Cochrane, Rohan spent the rest of the morning at Trail's End, checking on the huskies and talking to some of the dogsledders who'd arrived earlier. It wasn't a sport he'd ever been interested in, but speaking to the racers, he found himself intrigued.

When he asked about the chances of Phoebe training as a search and rescue dog, they looked a little skeptical.

"If she were trained from when she was a pup, then maybe, but huskies tend to have high prey drives, and that could be a distraction," one member named Ron said.

"And some are stubborn," his son, Tyler, added. "They don't always obey commands the first time around, and that's imperative in any type of emergency situation."

"She was part of a hoarding situation, and

I estimate her to already be over a year old," Rohan replied, somewhat disappointed.

"Well, there was that one guy, in Denmark I think, who was training his dog for SAR, remember, Dad? He was on one of the husky forums, sharing videos and talking about it."

Ron glanced back at Tyler and nodded.

"Yeah, I remember that, but he'd started training him from the time he got him at eight weeks old. It'll probably be very different with an older animal."

"Especially one who only just got a name," Rohan added. "She still doesn't even know it yet. She's smart, though. Where she is now, she's hanging out with a golden retriever, and she follows his cues."

"You should put together a sled team," the father said, but he chuckled as he said it, and Rohan joined in. "And if you're around in the next few days, I'll take you for a ride and teach you a little about the sport."

"Dad, it's Christmas. Dr. Khan's probably spending it with his family. Not everyone's as obsessed as we are."

Rohan was about to say, no, he had no one to spend the holidays with, then it struck him that he actually did.

The reality of it, the sweetness, sank in, making him smile.

"Yes, I'll be pretty busy with family, but maybe when my son comes home, I can bring him with me, if you're still here."

Just saying the words started a warm, silly glow in his chest, and he was grinning like an idiot as he excused himself to answer his phone.

It was Elise.

"Hi, I'm just about to make myself some lunch and wondered if you wanted anything."

There it was again, that feeling of hominess. Of domesticity.

Of rightness.

"I'd love some lunch," he replied, hearing the smile in his own voice.

"Oh," she said, as though surprised. "Well, it'll be ready in fifteen minutes."

"I'll leave here in a short time."

After they hung up, he said goodbye to the sled team and headed for his vehicle.

He knew why Elise had sounded so surprised at his upbeat tone. When he'd left that morning, he'd been curt and distant.

Elise had talked about the night before with such calm it was infuriating. She'd made it sound as if he was a dress she'd found at the back of her closet and, remembering how much she'd once liked it, wore it one last time, for old times' sake.

Fooling around.

Hearing her classify what they'd shared that way was like having ice water thrown in his face.

While she was perfectly sanguine about it, making love to Elise had opened a floodgate inside him, swamping him emotionally and mentally. Ratchetting the tension inside him tighter and tighter.

Yet she'd been right about the need to think only of Jeevan at this point, and putting much-needed distance between himself and Elise was the wisest thing to do. He had to think of her only as Jeevan's mother and nothing else, no matter how hard that was turning out to do.

The walls around his emotions had taken years to build, and seemingly had fallen in just one day, battered down by a woman he didn't remember, and a son he never knew he had.

During the night, while he looked at the photos, he'd found himself desperately searching for any memory, any hint of Elise, of the connection they'd shared. It was as though his brain insisted that before he could move forward, he had to remember the past.

Not hear about it. Not dissect it, as if it were something outside of himself, but actually *remember.*

The compulsion to search, to keep trying, was

driving him crazy, and being around Elise amplified the feeling.

How could he have loved her, made a baby with her, set out to alienate his family for her, and have no recollection of any of it?

How could she elicit so many feelings in him, and be, in every sense of the word, a stranger?

But when he'd realized he actually had family—one of his own—to spend the holidays with, there was no separation in his mind between her and Jeevan. They were to him a package deal, and he could see no way around it.

And although the thought was terrifying, it also filled him with satisfaction.

That was a dichotomy he wasn't willing to examine. While the sensible part of his mind tried to remind him of the need to be on guard against getting too involved with Elise, other parts of him were saying it was already too late.

When he got back to Elise's place, she was at the stove, making grilled cheese sandwiches. He inhaled the delicious scent of baked goods and eyed with interest the results lined up on the counter to cool.

"I got so caught up in the baking I almost forgot about lunch," she said. "I hope this is okay."

"You could just feed me some of those butter tarts instead," he replied, wanting to keep the conversation light. Spending the morning obsessively going over everything that had happened had been mentally exhausting, and he didn't think he could deal with any more serious conversations.

She sent him a look over her shoulder.

"So you still have a sweet tooth, eh?"

"Definitely," he replied, going to the sink to wash his hands as Baxter and Phoebe wound around his ankles, looking for his attention. He gave them both pets and rubs before squirting soap into his hand. "I think those look terrible, and I should try one of each to make sure they taste okay, before Jeevan has any."

That made her laugh and, when they sat down to eat, it was in a far less weighty atmosphere than the one in which they'd had breakfast.

As they ate, he told her about the conversation he'd had with the dogsled team members, and she told him about her phone call to the hospital.

"Ben's out of the ICU, and in a room, but they're still restricting visitors for the time being."

"Is that normal?" he asked, concerned for the young man's well-being.

She shrugged. "It depends. That could be on doctor's orders, or it could be a family request. If it's the former, they could be just particularly worried about infection, or keeping him undisturbed. He's listed as stable, and being out of

ICU makes me a little less worried about his prognosis."

"Before we leave to go shopping, we should check and see if he can have visitors yet."

She nodded. "Sure. I thought we could leave around three, which will give me a chance to finish up what I need to do here."

"So what can I do to help?"

"Untangle the lights for the tree," she said without hesitation. "They're a mess, and I lose patience with them. Every year I promise myself I'll put them away properly, and every year I end up just tossing them in the storage bin."

"Sure," he replied, glad to have something to do. "Should I put them on the tree, as well?"

"That would be amazing. I usually get Jeevan to do it, and then we put the ornaments on together. I thought we could take the boxes out this evening, and if he doesn't make it home tomorrow, you and I can decorate it so it's done when he gets in."

There she went again, making him feel as though this was all normal and he was an integral part of her life—and Jeevan's. Feeling ridiculously pleased, even as he reminded himself not to, he excused himself from the table and, after she said she'd wash their plates, took himself off to do battle with the lights.

* * *

Elise set about prepping for the Christmas Day meal, one ear open in case Rohan needed any help, but besides the occasional soft curse, he seemed to be handling the chore without too much fuss.

She shook her head, still trying to adapt to having him around, her wild swings in mood and attitude not helping.

Yesterday morning she'd been filled with rage when she realized he was still alive. That had morphed to sympathy and sadness when she realized the pain his accident had put him through. Traumatic brain injuries often left people floundering to figure out the world again, since the changes they wrought could manifest in a myriad of ways. Alterations in personality and loss of cognitive or physical function, along with long-term issues with fatigue and sensory overload could make patients and their families struggle to cope.

From what she remembered him telling her about his family, and what she'd found out over the past two days, Elise suspected Rohan hadn't had the support and understanding he needed. Yet he'd recovered and moved on with his life so well, and that filled her with admiration.

She didn't find herself grieving anymore for the man he'd been. Instead—far more dangerously—she was beginning to truly like and respect the man he was now.

As well as desire him.

So although she'd achieved her goal of putting a stop to any further amorous encounters with Rohan, it was a hollow victory. Sleeping with him hadn't extinguished her desire, only heightened it.

"Hey," he called from the other room. "Do you think Jeevan would be interested in going dogsledding? The team up at Trail's End invited me to come up and try it out, and when I said I'd be with family, they said I could come up after Christmas, and bring other people with me."

"He might," she said, tamping down a rush of unreasonable annoyance at being excluded. "He's pretty adventurous."

"Like his mother. Would you like to come, too?"

"Perhaps," she said, now exasperated with her own contrariness. Not two seconds ago she was fussing about being left out, and then, in the next moment, she was hiding behind a noncommittal response.

Of course, she wanted to go. Not because she was terribly interested in dogsledding, although it would be fun, but because she really wanted to spend more time with Rohan.

This new, enigmatic Rohan, who seemed

set to steal her heart all over again, once more against her will. However, whereas before she'd been afraid of love and abandonment, now she feared the effect on her son, and on Rohan. She never wanted him to think he had to be with her just so as to be able to see his son on a regular basis.

How was she going to manage being around him for the rest of the holidays? Even with Jeevan in attendance, it was going to take everything she had to stay sane and detached.

"Is Jeevan into sports?"

Rohan's question pulled her out of her own thoughts and made her realize she'd been operating on autopilot, instead of concentrating on what she was doing.

"Watching them or playing?" she called back.

"Either."

She heard the hunger behind the words, the need to start understanding his child, years and years later than he should have done. The pathos of it made her have to stop and catch her breath before she could reply.

"He's pretty athletic, so yes to both, really. He played hockey up until high school, and was pretty good. Used to skateboard and snowboard and, of course, ski. Oh, and he's a mean tennis player. I had to stop playing with him by the time he was in his midteens. It was getting embarrassing."

His soft laughter warmed her aching heart, and she wished she could see Rohan's face so she could know what he was thinking.

She waited for more questions as she worked, but he went silent, leaving her far too much time to think.

On a whim, she'd taken out the album she had of the two of them together, while he was out earlier. She didn't know what she was looking for, or hoped to find, but when she opened the cover tears prickled the backs of her eyes.

The love was there in every picture, every glance, each touch of one body against the next, whether just in the clasping of hands or an arm wrapped tightly around a waist.

On the final page in the album, she found the last picture she had of them together, taken in Toronto on the day before he left to go back to Trinidad. He'd taken her camera and asked a passer-by to take the shot as they stood outside the airport.

"You'll wait for me?"

He'd asked her that question at least twice before he left. While she'd said yes, she'd seen the skepticism in his eyes. She'd made no bones about not believing in love everlasting, but he'd sworn to make her change her mind, even if it took a lifetime.

And he had changed her mind, although not in the way he'd thought. From the first moment she held their son in her arms, she'd understood what it meant to know love that would never falter. Never die.

Of course, she hadn't waited for him for twenty-seven years. But looking at the pictures, she thought perhaps she'd been looking for someone who could make her feel the way he had and had never found that.

He wasn't the same, but she'd so easily stopped looking for signs of the old Rohan and just accepted the new, seeing the essence of the man she'd loved just beneath the cool veneer.

The twenty-seven-year-old Rohan had been supremely self-confident, or at least had given that impression. But she'd seen wariness in his eyes last night when she'd taken off his shirt, revealing the heartrending signs of what he'd been through. Had the accident knocked some of that bravado away, leaving him vulnerable in ways she'd never seen him be in the past?

How else had it changed him, deep inside?

And with all he'd been through the last day and a half, how was he truly coping?

She knew what the long-term effects of traumatic brain injuries could be. What emotional toll had yesterday's events taken on Rohan? Had what she saw as cold stoicism been a defense mechanism against feelings he didn't know how to handle or his brain wouldn't let him process properly?

If that were the case, was there anything she could do about it?

Or would he resent her for even trying?

"Hey, Elise," he called from the other room. "Do you have a knife, or a hand grenade?"

Laughter burst from her throat before she could stop it, and glad to have the tension ratcheting inside relieved, she grabbed a towel to wipe her hands, and headed into the living room.

"Don't go blowing up the house, Rohan."

"Well, it seems like a good option," he said, looking up as she entered the room. "Or I could buy new lights so I don't lose what's left of my mind trying to untangle this mess."

Her heart did a flip as her gaze met his laughing one, and it took all her power to not bend and kiss his smiling lips.

So instead, she frowned ferociously and plopped down beside him, holding out her hand.

"Give it here. I'll do it."

"Oh no," he said, moving it out of her reach. "*We* can do it, together."

CHAPTER FOURTEEN

His words stayed with her the rest of the afternoon, and although she tried not to dwell on them, she thought of them each time she looked at Rohan.

She was seeing him differently, she realized, as they walked to her truck to go into Banff. Before she'd been caught up in seeing the shadows and reflections of the young man she'd known. Now she saw the man he'd become and had no interest in comparing the two.

Not anymore.

Here was someone who'd weathered adversity, been blindsided by life when he'd least expected it, and somehow refused to break.

And she knew it was a struggle for him—had seen it for herself. Yet he kept it all together, and even though she had dropped the bombshell on him, raking up matters he no doubt would have preferred to stay in the past, he could smile and laugh, be silly with her.

She'd seen his outer scars and glimpsed his inner ones, but none of them held him back from accepting the idea of having a son. Indeed, he'd done so without protest, which was another mark in his favor.

Since Ben still wasn't allowed visitors, they went straight to the Banff Avenue shopping area.

It was ablaze with lights, which glinted off the snow even in the waning afternoon light, and festive decorations hung from every streetlamp and in all the store windows. Carolers, dressed like something out of a Dickens novel, walked among the shoppers, stopping periodically to serenade them.

"I know you said Christmas isn't your thing, and this is as festive as it gets," she told him as they strolled along. "But this is where the shopping is best. There's a suit store right over there."

"I'm actually enjoying this Christmas," he said, his voice casual. "For the first time in a very long time."

She didn't reply, as a wave of pleasure engulfed her, causing a lump in her throat.

At the clothing store, the sales woman was happy to help Rohan find a suit he liked, and that fit without needing alterations.

A little too happy, in Elise's estimation.

"This one is perfect," she all but purred, rubbing her hands across his shoulders from behind. "And the color really goes well with your skin tone."

Rohan turned to Elise, who was sitting on the sidelines, trying to appear unconcerned and hide her annoyance at the saleslady's over-the-top, touchy-feely pitch.

"What do you think?" he asked, raising his eyebrows. "Like it?"

"You look great," she said.

In reality, he looked fantastic.

Scrumptious.

Everything the saleslady said was true, but Elise knew firsthand exactly how the body beneath the fabric looked, and could see just how the navy-blue suit emphasized its best attributes. The jacket hung beautifully from his broad shoulders, and the dress pants did nothing to obscure his lean hips and wonderfully muscled thighs.

Just looking at him made her mouth water.

He'd picked out a light blue dress shirt and a blue tie with discreet red stripes, while a pair of black dress shoes completed the outfit.

The effect was both distinguished and sexy, and Elise realized how proud she was going to be, walking into the dinner with him the following night. Thank goodness she'd bought herself a new dress last week, instead of planning to trot out one of her "old faithfuls."

"I'll take it all," he told the beaming saleswoman.

Once they were back out on the main road, they took their time looking in the shop windows they passed.

Suddenly, Rohan paused in front of a gallery and said, "I want to go in here."

When she followed him in and saw what had caught his eye, she couldn't help smiling.

It was a small, stylized painting of a blue jay, done by a local artist whose name Elise recognized.

Rohan turned a questioning gaze her way. "Do you think Jeevan would like this?"

"I'm sure he'd love it," she replied, getting a little misty-eyed. "That's one of his favorite local artists, but he only has some prints, not an original."

Rohan immediately picked it up. "Plus, you said he likes corvids, right?"

"Right," she agreed as he went toward the cash register.

"Would you like this wrapped?" the gentleman manning the store asked.

"Yes, please," Rohan replied, adding, "It's for my son, and I would hate for it to get damaged."

Elise turned away so he wouldn't see how

touched she was, how much his words meant to her.

And how much she wanted him, right then.

Not just in a sexual way, but in every way she could think of. She could try to tell herself it was just echoes of love long gone that made her feel this way, but she already knew that wasn't true.

When she first fell for him, it was because of his sunny, winning disposition, his humor, along with his handsome face and young, fit body. While they'd had serious conversations, it was his open personality and the unfettered joy of him she remembered best.

He was still handsome despite his scars, and kept himself in good shape, but in many other ways he'd changed completely. There were flashes of humor now, not the constant smiling banter she'd so enjoyed. And he kept most of his thoughts and emotions to himself, when before they'd been freely shared, or visible in his expression.

Yet that didn't stop her from wanting him, just the way he was.

By the time the gift was wrapped, she had herself back under control, after a stern reminder that this wasn't about them, and Jeevan was their main—only—concern.

Outside, he looked up at the dark, cloudless

sky and remarked, "It's gotten colder. How about a coffee or hot chocolate, before we continue on?"

"Sure."

They waited for a horse-drawn carriage to pass, before crossing the busy street toward a café. As they stepped up on the sidewalk on the other side, a commotion broke out a few meters away.

"Hey, watch where you're going!"

"Mama? Mama?"

"Are you all right?"

"I think she's probably drunk."

At the cacophony of voices, Elise instinctively turned to see a young woman stagger to one side, putting out her hand to stop her momentum and steady herself against the building. It didn't help, as she lost her footing, going down in a heap.

A little girl standing nearby screamed, "Mama!" and rushed toward the fallen woman.

Elise was moving before she'd even thought about it, aware of Rohan coming up just behind. Getting to the woman, Elise parted the gathering crowd and said, "I'm a doctor. Let me through."

By the time she went down on her knees beside the woman, Rohan was coaxing away the little girl, who was crying for her mother.

Cursing the lack of her medical bag, Elise began her examination, although the woman weakly flailed with her right arm, as if trying to push her away, and mumbled unintelligibly.

"I'm calling an ambulance," Rohan said, his voice calm, controlled.

The woman's mumbling got louder, but Elise couldn't make out the words. She took her pulse, finding it rapid; the patient's breathing was shallow. Fear radiated from her eyes, which blinked and flickered as though she was having a hard time focusing.

And Elise saw a marked difference in her eyelids: the left one was drooping.

Perhaps an aneurysm or a stroke?

"It's okay," she said. Keeping the patient calm was imperative. There wasn't anything she could do out here on the sidewalk. They had to get her to a hospital ASAP. "Your daughter is safe, and I'm a doctor. Let me take care of you."

"Take my coat." Rohan handed it down, adding, "Ambulance is on the way."

Elise put Rohan's coat over the other woman, then held her hand, straining to hear the sound of sirens and heaving a sigh of relief when she heard them approaching.

"We're going to get you fixed up, okay?"

The chilled fingers squeezed slightly around Elise's, just as the emergency vehicle pulled up.

Looking up while digging her car keys out of her pocket, she said to Rohan, "I'm going to the hospital with her. Meet me there."

"Will do," he replied, still calm, the little girl now safely ensconced in his arms, her head on his shoulder, thumb in mouth. Bending, he took the keys from her hand. "You go and get her through this."

And somehow, the way he said it, with assurance of her abilities, made her feel like a million dollars.

Rohan had to hand the little girl, who'd told him her name was Brenna, over to the two police officers that attended on the scene, but Brenna wasn't happy about it.

The cops weren't happy, either, when the little girl started to wail.

"I'll come to the hospital," Rohan told her as she reached out her arms to him, after one of the officers had taken her from him.

"There's no need for that, sir," the other officer told him, sounding stern. "We'll take care of her until a relative can be found."

"I have to go there anyway," he responded. "I was shopping with Dr. van Hagan and I have to pick her up from the hospital."

Hearing Elise's name made them relax, and

neither objected again when he told Brenna he'd see her in a few minutes.

He hurried back to the truck and stowed the packages on the back seat. Suddenly realizing he didn't know where the hospital was, he had to take a moment to look it up with his GPS. Then, with the tinny voice giving him directions, he made his way there.

Going in through the front entrance, he paused, looking at the signs, trying to figure out where the emergency room waiting area was located. Following the arrows, he was about to make his way down a corridor when he spotted the gift shop.

Brenna was so scared. Maybe a stuffed toy or a book would make her feel a little bit better?

He went in and chose a virulently pink bunny and a picture book, after asking the lady at the register what would be appropriate for a three-year-old, which was his estimate of the little one's age.

Setting off, he took the corridor indicated, but soon realized he must have missed a turn. He'd just turned back when, from behind him, a voice said, "Jeevan! You're home early!"

But it was only when he felt a hand on his arm that he registered the woman dressed in scrubs was actually talking to him.

"I'm sorry," he said. "You've got the wrong person."

"Oh," she replied, looking both startled and chagrined, her gaze searching his face intently for an instant. "I'm so sorry. I thought you were someone else. Can I help you?"

As he walked away a moment later with the directions to where he needed to be, the knowledge of being a father struck him in a way it hadn't before.

Oh, he'd believed it, but until that nurse or doctor had mistaken him for his son, he'd thought of it in an almost academic way.

At one time, he and Elise van Hagan had been intimate, and that coupling had produced a child—Jeevan.

One plus one equaled two.

Nothing truly surprising about that, and because Rohan remembered nothing of his son's conceiving, Jeevan hadn't actually seemed real. Not even when he looked at the photographs, or heard Elise speak so lovingly of him.

But somehow, having the woman mistake him for his son brought the entire situation to life in a new way. Took it from the theoretical and made it completely, heartachingly factual.

It felt as though he were walking on air the entire way down to urgent care.

I'm a father. And my son looks like me.

As he was approaching the door to the waiting area, Elise came through another one farther down the hallway, and he went over to her.

"How is the patient doing?"

"She's holding her own, but I've called for a specialist."

"Elise. Rohan."

Hearing their names, they turned in unison to see Janice approaching from the opposite direction. She hugged them both, one after the other, as she got to them.

"How's Ben?" Elise asked.

"He's doing all right. Awake now after brain surgery and an operation to pin his leg. They've transferred him out of ICU into a room, and I just popped over to the cafeteria for a bite to eat." She smiled, but it didn't reach her tired, worried eyes. "He's not talking yet, but that's probably the effects of the anesthetic. Although the doctors keep talking about cognitive impairment, I'm sure he'll be fine. He'll be out of the hospital in no time."

The determination in her voice as she averred her son would recover worried him. He didn't want to frighten her, but at the same time, it was a situation too close to his own to let it pass.

"I'm sure he will, too," Rohan said gently. "But it might take some time."

"No, no." Her hand waved, as though telling

him to go away. "Ben's strong. He'll be fighting fit before we know it."

"I hope you're right. But head trauma can be tricky and take a while to heal." He found he'd raised his hand to his face and was tempted to drop it, but instead he lifted it higher, to the rear of his skull. "I know that from personal experience. And I know how frustrating it can be to be unable to rise to other people's expectations, when you're trying your best."

Janice's gaze searched his, and she nodded as tears filled her eyes.

There was nothing to do but put his arm around her shoulder and let her lean her forehead on his chest as she cried, probably for the first time since they'd got Ben out of the destroyed barn.

Looking over her head, he met Elise's gaze and found there an expression of such warmth that he had to look away. The conversation left him feeling exposed, vulnerable. He didn't want Elise's sympathy. In fact, he would go so far as to say that it was the last thing on earth he wanted.

But what she seemed to offer was understanding, and it almost undid him.

"Here," Elise said, thrusting some facial tissue into Janice's hand.

"Thank you." Janice stepped away, looking

a little ashamed. "I'm sorry for crying all over you like that, Rohan."

"You've had a long, stressful day," he said, then cleared his throat. "It's fine."

"I need to get back to Ben, but I'll remember what you said." She straightened her back, as though getting ready to do battle, but her lower lip quivered. "As a parent, sometimes you want the best for your child so badly that you push too hard, but I'll remember not to make Ben feel inadequate if he doesn't recover as quickly as I hope."

"That's the best thing to do for him, I think. Let him recover in his own time and support him as he does."

"I will," she said, giving them both quick hugs before heading for the elevators.

"That was good advice," Elise told him, her gaze warm, but probing.

"I hope she takes it," he admitted, knowing he was laying a painful part of his soul bare to her, and not caring anymore. "Or she could do more harm to Ben than good."

Someone popped their head out of a door and called for Elise.

"I have to go," she said before giving him the most heart-twisting smile and then hurrying off.

CHAPTER FIFTEEN

ELISE CAME OUT of the cubicle where her patient was, about ten minutes after she'd seen Rohan in the corridor. A glance into the emergency waiting area, to see where he was, had her heart aching with a combination of wonder and sorrow.

The patient's daughter, who was maybe two or three years old, was sitting sandwiched between Rohan and a police officer. She was clutching the rabbit she'd seen in Rohan's hand earlier, and the two men on either side of her were taking turns reading from the book perched on her lap.

That was the kind of father Rohan would have been to Jeevan: kind, gentle, willing to be involved. Knowing they'd both missed that opportunity was heartbreaking.

"That's your patient's daughter," a nurse said, following Elise's gaze. "Those two calmed her down and the man on her left even bought her that stuffie from the shop. They've been keeping her entertained while we try to figure out where the family is staying. She doesn't know the name of the hotel, but she did say her father is here with them."

Of course, Elise already knew most of that, but she made the nurse none the wiser.

"No sign of a room keycard in Mom's purse?"

"No, and her phone has one of those manual locks on the screen, where you have to know which pattern to draw before it'll let you in. I have one of the NAs calling the hotels, but it might take a while."

"Mom's had a minor stroke," Elise said. "And I've called for a neurosurgeon to consult, so we need to find Dad ASAP."

"We're doing our best," the nurse advised.

"I'll see if I can find out anything useful from the daughter," Elise said as the nurse hurried away.

Taking a deep breath, Elise made her way over to the little group, and she almost faltered when Rohan looked up and saw her—and smiled.

It was the kind of smile that was almost a grin, and did all kinds of crazy things to her body and her heart. Once more, in an inappropriate place, she wanted to grab him and kiss him.

Ignoring her reactions was almost impossible, but she had to put them aside.

Until later, at least.

Stooping down in front of the little girl, she said, "Hi, I'm Elise. What's your name?"

"Brenna," the little one replied. "Wanna read my book wif me?"

"I'd like that, but maybe later, okay?" Elise smiled, glad the men had already put Brenna at ease, which would make asking her questions that much simpler. "But first, can you tell me what you, your mom and dad have done since you got here?"

Brenna scrunched her forehead and then said, "We played in the snow and petted the aminals. There was a donkey and some goats and a bunny like mine." She held up the object in question. "But the bunny was white, not pink."

"The George's Inn, out by Chester Road, has an indoor petting zoo," the policeman said quietly. "I've taken my kids out there a time or two."

Elise nodded. She'd come to the same conclusion, too, when Brenna spoke. She got up and touched the little girl's hair. "I'll get them to try there. Thank you, Brenna."

But even while she was giving instructions for someone to call the inn, it was the image of Rohan reading to Brenna and the beauty of his smile that stuck in Elise's mind.

The smile, in particular, had thrown her system into overdrive. There was something different about it, but she couldn't put her finger on what the difference had been.

All she knew was that it had set her senses on fire and made the wanting she'd been fighting all day almost impossible to subdue.

But they'd agreed that Jeevan had to come first, and their relationship, whatever it became, was far lower on the list of priorities. Some might say Jeevan was a grown man and should be able to handle anything that came along, but Elise refused to put him in a position to have to choose between his parents.

He was, and had to continue to be, her first consideration.

Nothing else could be allowed to matter.

Not Rohan, who increasingly took up more of her headspace than was wise and had the ability to turn her inside out with a look, a word, a shared confidence.

And not her own selfish desires.

"I found him, Dr. van Hagan." The NA put down the phone. "Mrs. Pilar's husband is on his way here."

"Excellent," she said, gathering up her chart and heading back to the cubicle to check on the patient. "Please call upstairs and ask for an ETA for the neurosurgeon."

But she couldn't resist one more glance into

the waiting room, and could only smile, heart melting, at the sight of Rohan holding the shocking pink bunny and pretending it was reading.

And once more she experienced a wave of anger as she realized all she and Jeevan had lost, the day Rohan went back to Trinidad.

But that was dangerous, too, she knew, because there was no way to go back and change the past, and to hanker for something that never was, and never could be, was unhealthy.

Best to be thankful for the present and not wish for anything more than what she already had.

With that bracing yet somehow depressing thought, she hurried back to her patient.

By the time Elise handed off Mrs. Pilar to the incoming doctor and neurosurgeon, Brenna's father had arrived, and Rohan was released from his babysitting job.

Brenna hugged him tight as her father thanked him, over and over, and Rohan just said it was fine.

The truth was, though, interacting with Brenna had been a joy, not a chore, and had made him happy and sad in turns. It had made him think that perhaps he might have been a decent father to a child that age, although he completely understood spending a couple of hours with her wasn't really a good indication.

He was still on a high from being confused for Jeevan at the hospital, too. Although to anyone else it might seem silly, for him it was a true turning point. Yet part of him hesitated to share the moment with Elise, wanting to hug it to himself a little longer.

As he and Elise walked to the pickup, she said, "Thanks for sitting with Brenna." Her smile just increased his sense of well-being. "She must have been so scared."

"She was, and the police officer was doing his best to console her, but it wasn't working."

They got into her truck and were fastening their seat belts. Elise's smile softened into something so sweet, so glorious he couldn't help staring. Staring and wanting.

He wanted to kiss it off her lips, feel her mouth go from smiling to passion-filled.

Dragging his eyes away from her face, he fumbled with the buckle, getting it latched just as she put the vehicle into gear.

"The bunny and book were masterstrokes. Which female can resist something soft and fuzzy, and having two men cater to her?"

He tried to laugh, but it was a rusty sound, roughened by his lust for the woman beside him.

Stop it. Behave. That's not what any of this is about.

But the self-chastisement did nothing to tamp down his desire. Only the habits and control of years kept his hands unmoving on his lap, and his mind firmly on the conversation.

"Will her mother be okay?"

"I can't discuss the specifics with you, but I think in time she will."

She sounded grim, and he wondered what had happened.

"Can you at least tell me if it were a substance abuse issue or physical disease?"

She sent him a sidelong look, then sighed. "Disease."

Probably neurological then, or perhaps a diabetic episode. Whatever it was, Rohan was glad that sweet little girl's mother hadn't been drunk or on drugs.

"Home now, I think, to get something to eat," she said. "I'm getting hungry again."

"Why don't we get some dinner here in Banff?" She'd been busy all day, and he didn't like the thought of her going home and having to cook.

"It might be hard to find somewhere that isn't full, although… There's one place that might find us a table."

He wondered at her hesitation but realized

the source when they got to the small restaurant, which was full, and the hostess came out from behind her podium.

"Dr. van Hagan, welcome! It's been ages. Dad will be so happy to see you."

She immediately led them to a secluded table, chattering away about her family. Not long after she left to get their drinks, a gentleman in a chef's uniform came out of the kitchen and made a beeline for them.

"Dr. Elise." When she got up to greet him, she was enveloped in a huge hug. "This lady saved my son's life," he said, loud enough for some nearby patrons to hear.

Elise blushed and tried to downplay it.

"It was a team effort, Mr. Kitterly."

But he was having none of it.

"If you weren't there, on the slopes where you found him, he wouldn't have made it. The surgeons told me so."

By the time he left to go back to the kitchen, Elise was beet red.

"His son was an excellent skier," she said, grabbing her menu and not meeting Rohan's gaze. "Was a world-class athlete before his accident. It's such a shame."

"You did a lot of good in SAR. Why are you embarrassed when people acknowledge that?"

"I didn't do it for the accolades," she said, adding a little huff for good measure.

"Why did you do it?" he asked, keeping his voice gentle.

She sighed and put down the menu. "It was actually all I ever wanted to do, from the time I was a little girl and saw a documentary about a SAR team. But like I said, my mom talked me out of it because she didn't think I could make a living if that was all I did."

Rohan considered that for a moment, waiting until a waiter had brought their drinks and left again. Then he said, "It's a shame you decided to give it up. I know your capabilities, firsthand, even after you've been away from it for a year."

He saw the anguish in her eyes as she leaned forward to say, "But even yesterday, I froze. That can't happen during a rescue."

"But it did," he said, mildly. "Then you un-froze and continued on, rescuing a young man who might have died if you hadn't acted as de-cisively as you did, and saving a dog's life, too. Even though you must have been terrified, you got the job done."

She stared at him, eyes wide and luminous, and his breath caught in his throat at her beauty.

When he could speak again, he said, "I think it was Nelson Mandela who said, 'Courage is not the absence of fear, but the triumph over it.'

You've triumphed, and I think you would again, if you wanted to."

"Like you did," she said, taking him off guard at the swift change of subject.

"What do you mean?"

"I heard what you told Janice this evening, and I remember the things you said about your family when we were young. I can only assume you didn't get the support and understanding you needed after your accident. Not everyone would be able to thrive the way you have, after going through all that."

"Thrive?" He would laugh, but the bitterness surrounding the subject made it stick in his throat. "I don't know that what I've been doing over the last few years could be categorized that way."

Just then the waiter came back, and they ordered, Rohan choosing quickly, since he'd hardly looked at the menu. He was hoping once the young man was gone, Elise would change the subject, but she went right back to their prior discussion.

"You don't consider being a partner in a business, doing what you've always loved, as thriving?"

"Maybe on a materialistic level," he said, even as he wondered why he was compelled to speak so frankly about it. "But socially, I've distanced myself. My coping mechanisms aren't very…friendly. When I'm having a hard time, I retreat. Hide in my head. It destroyed my marriage, because Suvarna couldn't deal with it."

She nodded, the sympathy in her eyes almost more than he could stand. He never talked about it, but somehow he wanted—*needed*—her to understand.

"I would have liked to give her what she wished for, but my remoteness, the wall between me and the world, which included her, was just too large. I couldn't connect emotionally, and the harder she pushed the further I stepped back. If I feel as though things are out of my control, or if I'm stressed, I back all the way up until I can regroup."

"I've noticed that. But at the same time, you pull yourself out of it and start communicating when you're ready." She smiled slightly, her gaze warm on his. "That's the important part, isn't it?"

"Is it?" he rebutted, his chest aching. "I want to connect with my son, not shut him out if he asks the hard questions."

"Just…be you," she answered quickly. "He isn't a child without any experience of the world. Don't pretend to be anything you're not comfortable with, and he'll accept you as you are."

"How do you know that?" he asked, with

fierce swiftness. "How can you know how he'll react?"

She took a deep breath.

"Because he already loves you, even though he thinks you're deceased. I raised him to. I wanted him to know who his father was, and what a good man he was. Jeevan will accept that you're older, maybe a little sterner than I described you. But from his perspective, the emotion is already implanted. All you have to do is accept it."

Rohan froze, his fingers clenched so fiercely together they began to ache. Elise put her hand over his, and the warmth that flowed between them made his chest tighten with a mixture of pleasure and pain.

"How could I have forgotten you, Elise? Loved you and then wiped the memory from existence?"

He hadn't meant to ask, but the words were out before he could stop them. She shrugged, and although there was a hint of sorrow in her eyes, she looked serene, at peace.

"That wasn't your fault, Rohan. The brain is a complex organ, and no matter how hard you try, once the damage is done, it's rare it can ever be reversed. Just…put that aside as something we have to accept and move forward from."

"We?" He shot the question at her, not angrily but in surprise.

"Yes, *we*. Don't you think I've been struggling to deal with that, too? It hurts, deep down, that you didn't know me, have no recollection of the time we spent together. But I know it wasn't willful on your part, that it was a side effect of an event that still haunts you, and I'm coming to terms with it. You've had longer to accept it, but I get the feeling you never have."

He looked away, letting his gaze roam the room, seeking some modicum of calm before facing her again.

"I avoided thinking about it, for a long time. When the internet became more accessible, I was still trying to figure out where I was, and what I was doing during those lost months. I contacted old schoolmates, friends I hadn't seen in years, and asked them if they knew. When no one seemed able to give me an answer, I think I decided I'd never know."

He paused, shook his head. "But the hole—the gap—in my memory banks was a constant ache, one I've never been able to soothe. And now it hurts even more, because I know if I could find the piece of my memory that's missing, it would have you in it. You, and your love, and the joy we shared together."

Now it was she who looked down, as though

hiding. It popped into his head to say that perhaps they could find that love and joy again, but he bit the words back, frightened by the impulse.

Hearing her admit she was struggling with his amnesia, too, somehow made his own fight a little more bearable, and the whole situation sadder.

While he was oblivious to the emotional nuances, she would remember everything. All the little gestures, the inside jokes, the patterns they'd formed together. After all these years he knew she didn't still love him the way she had. To think she might would be ludicrous. Yet no doubt some of the old emotions would linger, causing her additional hurt.

And causing her to make love with him, as she had the night before.

But he couldn't afford to think about that, since she'd made it clear a repeat wasn't in the cards.

So he was relieved when the waiter approached with their food and put an end to the conversation.

CHAPTER SIXTEEN

WHEN THEY LEFT the restaurant, they were both quiet, lost in their own thoughts, and Elise decided not to pursue any deep conversation again.

She felt raw, ragged around the edges, and unable to cope.

It had become clear to her as they spoke that she was falling for Rohan again, and she didn't know what to do. What she really wanted was time to think, but with Jeevan hopefully on his way home and Rohan staying at her house, there really wasn't any. Not the kind of solid alone time she needed.

When they got to the house, it was too early to go to sleep, so she said, "Want to play some cribbage?"

He smiled, but it was just a tiny upturn of his lips. "I haven't played in years, but sure."

Playing cards was definitely preferable to getting back to their discussion.

She lit the fire, and they set up the cribbage

board on the hearth rug. Rohan seemed lost in thought, and because he wasn't concentrating, she beat him around the board the first time, and when he called for a rematch, she beat him again.

The nice thing was that as they played, they talked. Not about heavy subjects like amnesia or surprise parenthood, but about their lives and jobs, where they'd worked, and how they'd ended up where they were.

"I would have pegged you more for a Toronto type of guy," she said, being honest. "You used to love the city."

He shrugged. "I started out there when I first moved back, but just found myself drifting farther and farther west. When I got to Calgary, it felt good, so that's where I've been for about eight years."

"I moved here from there about twelve years ago, when my sister and her husband went to Vancouver. I wanted to try my hand at search and rescue, and this was a great place to volunteer."

Simple, easy conversation, but the entire time she was so aware of his every move, gesture and breath. There was something compelling about him that she found almost irresistible.

Before they started a third match, she went

into the kitchen and came back with a plate of Christmas treats.

"Oh," he all but groaned with delight. "Those look delicious."

She grinned. "Just a few lemon squares, Nanaimo bars and butter tarts to tempt you."

He took a bite of a butter tart and closed his eyes as though in ecstasy.

After he swallowed, he said, "I just remembered, someone at the hospital mistook me for Jeevan from behind."

Elise watched his expression and asked, "What did you do?"

He shrugged as his hand hovered over the plate, while he decided between a lemon square and a Nanaimo bar.

"Told her she was mistaken. But I have to admit, it brought everything home to me in a way just talking about him hadn't."

She didn't want to go back to serious conversation, she was having way too much fun just chatting and laughing with Rohan. It was, in many ways, just like the old days, although she didn't want to tell him that, in case the reminder of his amnesia caused a resurgence of his stress.

But there was something bothering her, and she vacillated between saying something and letting it lie. He'd spoken with such sadness about his experiences with his family after the accident, and she remembered how upset he'd been when he discovered how his father and Chandi had acted.

That kind of anger ate away at you, and she hated the thought of him carrying it in his heart.

As they finished the third cribbage match, she said, "Are you still angry about what happened all those years ago?"

"How can you ask me that?" He gave her a fierce glare. "Of course I am."

She held his gaze, feeling his pain and sympathizing.

"I think," she said slowly, "you should forgive your family."

The look he gave her could have felled an oak, but she didn't look away, refusing to back down.

"What they did was unforgivable."

He said it with such finality she almost gave up. But at the same time, she knew she couldn't.

"True," she agreed. "Do it anyway. For your sake and Jeevan's. Don't you think he's going to want to meet your side of his family at some point?"

"Yes, but—"

"What are you going to do if you take him to meet them? Cherry-pick who he gets to talk to, and who gets greeted with a glare?" She shook her head and continued softly, "When this all sinks in, he'll have anger enough of his own to deal with, don't you think? Why add yours on top of it?"

"He has a right to be angry. We do, too. Aren't you angry, Elise?"

"Sure." She fiddled with the cribbage pegs, trying to find the right words, giving her hands something to do to stop them from reaching for him. She wanted so badly to touch him, hold him so as to ease his agony, but she didn't dare. Her emotions were too close to the surface, her desire for him too strong.

"Part of me is livid about the entire situation. But realistically, none of that anger will give me back any of what I'm upset about losing. It won't let Jeevan have his father growing up, or give me back a minute with you, or stop you from being in the accident. So what's the use of holding on to it and letting it rule my life? Worse, why pass it on to Jeevan?"

"You can forgive my father and Chandi, and just move on?" He shook his head. "That's crazy. I can't do it."

It came back to her, in one of those full-circle moments life occasionally tosses up. She looked over at him to say, "I'll tell you what you once told me: 'I don't know what forces in his life caused your father to act the way he did, but sometimes you have to accept people are the way they are, and there's nothing you can do about it.'"

He'd been lounging on his side, one hand propping up his head, but now he sat up, curiosity sharpening his gaze.

"When did I say that?"

"After I told you about my father abandoning us when I was small, and never looking back once he left."

She took a deep breath, trying to hold on to her composure. "When we met, my mother had only been dead for a few years, and I was still grieving. You asked me about my father, and I told you he'd taken off when I was eight. What you said to me that night helped me realize I really didn't know the full story, so a few years later, Emma and I did some research. We couldn't find our father, but we located a sister of his, and she explained that our father had mental health issues since he was a child. Medication would help for a while, and then either stop having any efficacy or he'd come off it, thinking he was cured.

"She hadn't seen him in decades. He'd just taken off one day, and none of his family heard from him again, just like what had happened with us. We all figure that his need to disappear is part of the pathology of his disease, but that doesn't make it any easier to deal with, especially when I don't know what ultimately happened to him."

"I'm sorry for all you and your sister went through." He brushed the back of her hand with his, and the jolt of electricity she felt up her arm was way beyond what she should, with such a gentle touch.

"I didn't tell you that to get sympathy. I told you so you'd understand how hard it was for me when I thought you'd died. It was like being abandoned all over again, and I grieved like any one would, including getting angry with you. But the truth was, you were the father of my child, and I had to forgive you so I could raise him to be proud of who he is, and where he came from. I could have poisoned him against you with my grief and anger, but I refused to do that. Don't poison him against your family with yours."

He looked into the fire as though unable to meet her gaze a moment more, and he shook his head but said, "I'll think about it, but I can't promise I'll be as magnanimous as you are."

And with that she had to be content.

Rohan watched Elise get up, her fluid movements reminding him of her strength and flexibility. Remembering other ways those attributes had been displayed caused a rush of heat up his spine, and he turned his gaze back to the fire, to hide the desire he was sure was reflected in his eyes.

As she walked around the room and turned on the Christmas lights, which they hadn't bothered with before, she said, "I'm going to make some tea. Do you want some? Or coffee?"

Getting himself under control, he turned to her with a smile. "Coffee would be great, thank you."

He was starting to understand her, he realized, watching with frank appreciation the swing of her hips as she went out the door. After one of these deep, uncomfortable conversations, she wanted to get up and move. Find something to do. Be active, even in a small way. As if by doing so she was able to release some of the stress or digest all that had been said.

God, he was lucky to have her as the mother of his child.

Somehow she'd been able to shelve her own pain and anger and raise Jeevan to love a man he'd never met, and—as far as they knew at the time—had no chance of meeting.

Rohan still got those washes of hot and cold in his belly each time he thought about meeting his son, but now they heralded more excitement than trepidation.

Not that all his fears had been put to rest. But

at least now he had good reason to hope they would be able to forge a bond.

No pressure, though. Not from Rohan's side. It had to be at least somewhat organic.

Titan whistled and the bell in his cage, put there for stimulation, rang wildly for a few seconds, then went silent. Rohan looked his way, and the parrot bobbed up and down on his perch, doing a little dance.

"Good birdie," Titan said, tilting his head to one side and then the other. "Pretty Titan."

"You're a ham," Rohan told him, chuckling, and realizing how easily the laughter came in the moment.

It wasn't always like that, for him, and especially after the emotional wringer he'd been through, it felt strange, but good. The simple pleasure of amusement filled him with calm contentment. Being with Elise eased the pain he always carried in his heart, lightened his soul.

Had it been that way before? Somehow he thought it might have been. He could imagine speaking to her about his father and having his anger and discontent at their relationship leached away. He'd never know for sure, but he knew loving her had given him the courage to face his father head-on, when in the past he'd have been more subtle, or just given in for a peaceful life.

Elise's phone rang, and he heard the murmur of her voice from the other room. Figuring she'd be a while, Rohan looked around for something to divert his thoughts away from her, and his ever-present desire to kiss her, make love to her again.

The photo albums were on the coffee table, and he reached over and took the one off the top. He felt better equipped to look at them now than he had been last night. Then he'd been a mess of tangled, shocking emotions, while today he was steadier, mentally stronger.

Then he opened the cover and froze.

These weren't pictures of Jeevan, but of him and Elise.

Younger. Oh, so heartbreakingly young, but smiling at each other with the kind of love that was unmistakable.

Without conscious thought his hand went to the scarred side of his face as he looked at a photo of himself with unmarked, unblemished skin. When he realized what he was doing, he let his fingers fall away again and rode out the painful moment.

Elise had said everyone changed as they got older, and Rohan realized she'd accepted him as he was, now, just as she had in the past. Somewhere along the line, he'd forgotten that self-acceptance was important, and had continued to resent all the changes the accident had brought.

Seeing himself as he used to be helped Rohan reconcile himself to the loss of the young man staring into the camera and be okay with the older, hopefully wiser one he had become.

Flipping the pages one by one, he realized something else. Something that had him going back to the beginning, and taking another, closer look.

His heart started to race, disbelief making him flip back and forth through the album. What he was seeing made no sense, and yet there it was, right in front of him. As far as he was concerned, there could be only one explanation that made any sense and, in doing so, account for everything he'd been feeling about Elise.

"That was Jeevan on the phone." Elise walked in carrying a tray, which she put down on the table. "He's finally got a flight out of Hong Kong, but he won't be here until Christmas morning."

Rohan looked up at her, and he didn't know what she saw in his expression, but it made her abandon the drinks and kneel beside him on the rug.

Putting her hand on his shoulder, she asked, "What's wrong?"

"It might sound weird," he said, his voice suddenly hoarse from the lump that had gathered in his throat. "But I think I've been looking for you."

Her hand fell away and she leaned back, as though distancing herself from his words.

"What?"

"I've been looking for you since I returned to Canada. Not consciously, but everywhere we went twenty-seven years ago, I've been to since I came back."

She shook her head. "That does sound weird. You're just imagining it."

He didn't know why, but her down-to-earth common sense just made him even surer.

Pointing to a picture, he said, "This is Corner Brook, Nova Scotia, isn't it?"

She looked at the photo and slowly nodded. "I think so."

"And that's Tignish, PEI. That one is Truro, and this one—" he flipped a few pages "—this one is Moncton. I know, because about fifteen years ago, I decided I wanted to travel through the Maritimes. I didn't know why, but I felt compelled to go. I went to all those spots, plus Halifax and Quebec City." He found the pictures of those cities, pointing them out to her. "Then, the following year, I spent a month in Algonquin Park, canoeing and camping."

"Rohan, it could be just a coincidence." Elise sat cross-legged beside him, a wary look in her eyes. "A bizarre one, but a coincidence all the same."

"I don't think so. After I'd worked in Toronto for a while and made those trips, I got restless and decided to move. The first place I lived after that was Guelph."

"Not surprising, since you went to school there, and it would be familiar."

He shook his head. "I still wasn't satisfied. I kept moving, farther west each time, staying a year, sometimes less, until I got to Calgary. Then I stopped. Why, after years of wandering, did I stop there, if not because I knew, deep inside, that was where you came from, and probably would be?"

CHAPTER SEVENTEEN

ELISE STARED AT ROHAN, taking in the smile on his face, the gleam in his eyes. It was like seeing a mask fall away to reveal someone you'd known long ago and never thought to see again.

Despite the scars, he looked like the man he'd been twenty-seven years ago.

And it frightened her on a visceral level, as did what he was saying.

Surely he didn't believe he'd been subconsciously trying to find her for almost twenty years?

"You're talking crazy, Rohan. That makes no sense."

His smile actually widened. "It makes perfect sense to me, Elise. Why else would I find myself drawn to you in a way I can't remember ever being attracted to anyone else before? And last night, when we made love, why did it feel so natural, so incredibly intimate? I think…we were made to be together. And no matter what we do, we'll always find our way back to each other."

She shook her head vehemently, the fear in her belly churning, making her nauseous. "I don't believe that. That's not how memory, how the brain works."

Tipping his head to the side, he surveyed her with a look so loving it almost was her undoing. "Didn't you say the brain was a complex organ? Why wouldn't something as important to me as the love we shared be stored somewhere, even if the memories of us being together were lost?"

"I don't know, but I won't believe you've been searching for me, or that there's still a connection between us other than the past, or nostalgia, and the fact we have a son together. That's all nonsense."

Yet a part of her wanted to believe it, desperately. She couldn't let it overwhelm her, in case he decided, sometime later, he'd made a mistake and leave her again.

A few strands of her hair had come loose, and he slid them behind her ear with his fingers. She gasped, heat fanning out from where he touched, the familiar gesture making the conversation that bit more surreal.

"I don't remember any of that past, so I can't be nostalgic about it, and I know your reactions to my touch are from more than just good memories. Why are you afraid?"

She couldn't articulate it, terror holding her vocal cords hostage.

The specter of loving, of giving her all only to once more be abandoned arose in her mind, and she whispered, "Stop, Rohan. Please don't…"

He reached for her, and she wanted to resist but couldn't. Instead, she found herself collapsing, almost boneless, into his embrace, craving the security of his arms as much as she feared him going away, never to return.

"When we're like this, how can you doubt we should be together?" he whispered into her ear, sending shivers along her spine. "We still fit perfectly—the way those pictures show we always have."

How could she explain? All day they'd spoken of his fears, especially about being a father to Jeevan, but they'd only briefly touched on her own.

Then he said, "Are you afraid I'll leave you again, like I did before?"

She lifted her head to search his expression, tears threatening again at the tenderness in his eyes.

And it was that gentle regard that gave her the courage to reply, "Yes."

His arms tightened around her, and he bent

to place a gentle, loving kiss on her lips before resting his forehead against hers.

"I don't blame you. I promised to be back for Christmas, and it took me twenty-seven years to keep my word. I wouldn't trust me, either, under those circumstances. How about we take it slow, date for a while, so you have time to learn to trust me again? Even if you never do, I'll always be here for you. I don't plan to desert you again."

"And what do we tell Jeevan? I don't want him to be hurt by whatever we do."

"He's an adult now. I think he'll probably understand that there's still something special between us, but we're not going to rush into anything. And we can make sure he knows he'll never have to choose between us. We'll both always be around for him, whenever he needs."

Elise tried to call on her steady head and common sense so as to make the right decision, but the conflict in her mind was too strong. One part wanted to immediately agree to take one more chance on loving Rohan Khan, but another part insisted on caution. Loving him had almost broken her, had left scars that, although they weren't visible, still ached deep in her heart.

Could she really risk it all again?

Then she remembered all the advice she'd

given Rohan during the day, about leaving the past behind and moving forward in life. While he'd been stuck because of his accident, she'd been too afraid to risk being hurt again.

It was time to break free from the past, for both her and Rohan, and maybe they could, over time, heal each other with love and forgiveness.

She took a deep gulp of air, for courage, and said, "I'd like to try your idea of dating, although it's a bit of a haul from Calgary to here and back."

Rohan gave her a squeeze and she heard him blow out a breath, as though he'd been holding it in while she deliberated.

"An hour and a half isn't too long a drive. But I have all that accumulated vacation time, too. I could book a hotel room here for a couple of weeks. Give us a chance to figure out how we want to arrange things."

Leaning back slightly, she looked up at him. "Why not just stay here?"

His eyebrows rose. "In the spare room?"

She shook her head. "No."

"What about Jeevan? I thought you didn't want to give him any ideas about us getting together?"

"Honestly, it's time I stop using him as an excuse not to have a life. And I think it would be good for him to see us try, even if eventually we decided it isn't working. After all, he's heard me say all his life what a wonderful man you are. If I let you get away again, he's going to think either I'm a liar or a fool."

Rohan laughed, and her heart sang to once more see a glimpse of his old self, which before had been so overshadowed by the cold mask he wore.

That deep, joyous laughter, more than almost anything else, gave her additional hope for the future. If they could talk and laugh and love, share their fears and their dreams like they had so long ago, everything would come right in the end.

Reaching up, she cupped his still-smiling face in her hands and, with her heart full of thankfulness for the second chance they'd so miraculously been given, laid her lips gently on his. When he pulled her closer, deepening the kiss, she allowed herself to let go of the past and all its attendant pain so as to be completely and totally present with Rohan.

The Rohan of now, and hopefully her future.

They made love in front of the fire, slowly, his tenderness almost moving her to tears.

He touched her as though she were the most precious thing in the world, kissed her as though he never wanted to stop.

"You're so beautiful," he told her, his hands

cupping her face, his eyes gleaming in the fire-light.

"So are you," she told him, tracing his lower lip with her finger.

They caressed with long, leisurely strokes, taking their time as they relearned each other's bodies. Somehow, now that they'd come to this point, the rushed intensity of the night before wasn't necessary. They could spend as long as they wanted and needed, letting their passions build.

But the power of that desire was immense, and Elise whimpered, caught on the almost painful line between arousal and culmination.

And when he tipped her over into ecstasy, she cried out and hung on to him as if she would never let him go.

This time, when they were satiated, she didn't roll away but curled up beside him, her head on his arm. He was facing her, his hand on her hip, their legs intimately intertwined.

"I wish I'd seen you pregnant with Jeevan," he said, a touch of melancholy in his tone. "Or found you sooner, so we could have had more children."

Rubbing her hand over his chest, she said, "No regrets. We're looking ahead now, not back."

"I know, but— What the—"

He sat up so suddenly Elise was left lying in a confused heap, having banged her head on the floor. When she sat up, it was to see Rohan glaring at Baxter, who was standing next to them, a querulous expression on his shaggy face. Phoebe stood in the doorway, keeping her distance, yet very much interested in what was going on.

"He…he *goosed* me," Rohan accused. "And his nose is damned cold."

Elise tried to tell him that was Bax's way of reminding them it was way past his walkies time, but she started giggling instead, and couldn't stop. Rohan's outrage, when he turned his accusatory look from the dog to her, just made it worse.

Finally, as though unable to help himself, Rohan joined in, his laughter ringing through the house, sweet to her ears.

Baxter stalked off, obviously unimpressed.

Getting to her feet, still giggling, she started putting back on her clothes.

"Where are you going?" Rohan grumbled.

"The dogs need to go out," she replied.

Rohan yawned and stretched, then grabbed his jeans before rising also.

"I'll go with you," he said.

Once they had on their outerwear, Elise turned on the light above the back door and let the dogs out. As she followed with Rohan, he reached out to take her gloved hand in his, and something about that simple gesture melted away the last of her fears.

Except for what would happen when Jeevan got home.

As though sensing the change in her mood, Rohan squeezed her finger.

"Any regrets?"

"None," she answered honestly. "Just a little worried about how what's happening between us will affect Jeevan."

"I am, too," he admitted, as they watched Phoebe and Bax play a game of Keep Away in the snow. "We'll take it slowly, as we agreed, although I have to tell you, it won't be easy."

"Why not?"

He turned to look at her, and even in the low light from the single bulb, she could see the gleam of rekindled desire in his eyes.

"Because just looking at you makes me want you," he said, low and sweet. "And I don't know how to stop the entire world knowing that, whenever we're together."

What had happened to the stern, stoic man? The one who'd admitted to locking his feelings away and retreating from entanglements?

When she asked him as much, he snorted, the

sound one of laughter and bemusement combined.

"I have no idea. Over the past two days, he's slowly faded away. Not that I think I'll revert to the person I used to be before the accident. Just that somehow the burden of the past, the weight of it, seems to have lifted."

"I'm glad," Elise said, "if it makes you feel better. But there's nothing wrong with taking a step back—mentally, or emotionally—if you're uncomfortable in a situation or conversation. That ability has helped you through the years, and it's a good one to have."

He turned his face up to the night sky, inhaling deeply. Then he dropped her hand and put his arm around her waist, pulling her in tight against his side.

When he spoke, his voice was little more than a whisper.

"For years I've believed the man I am now is far inferior to the one I was. People told me so, over and over, and I absorbed that, like a slow-acting poison."

He turned, guiding her around, so they were face-to-face. His expression of wonder, of joy, made tears gather in her eyes.

"You've given me the antidote I needed, and I'll always be infinitely grateful for that."

He pulled her in closer and kissed her, their

lips going from chilled to hot between one breath and the next.

There was no need for more words between them, so she called the dogs in, and led Rohan straight to her bed. Although nothing had been completely settled, she knew, if she had her way, there would be very few nights that they slept apart going forward.

Yet as she tried to drift off in Rohan's arms, the worry that Jeevan might find all this unfathomable held sleep in abeyance.

Jeevan was a scientist through and through. The type of man who needed evidence to support any theory. Elise, who was the same way, couldn't help thinking that he'd find the events of the last days crazy.

If anyone had come to her with a story like the one she would have to tell their son, she'd caution them to be careful, to make sure they weren't letting old emotions cloud their judgment.

It was what she'd told herself, over and over, since recognizing Rohan, but now it couldn't sway her from the course she was on.

"You okay?" He asked it gently, stroking her arm. The soft caress unraveled the tension that had built inside, and as she kissed the soft skin on the inside of his elbow, the last of it melted away.

She loved him, and everything would come right in the end.

"Perfect," she replied.

He tugged her closer, so her back was snug against his chest, and, cocooned in his warmth, she fell asleep.

CHAPTER EIGHTEEN

THE NEXT MORNING, awaking with Elise still wrapped securely in his arms had Rohan smiling before he'd even gotten out of bed.

When she rolled over and wrapped her leg over his, while pulling his head down for a kiss, his happiness turned to passion and eventually to ecstasy.

They took the dogs out together, holding thermal coffee mugs in their mittened hands. Clouds were massed on the horizon, although the weather service said there would be no more snow until late that night.

He knew Elise was worried when he caught her staring westward, where the weather system would come from.

"He'll make it," he said, not needing to elaborate.

That drew a smile. "I'm sure he will."

But a little shadow of concern lingered in her eyes.

To cheer her up, he put down his cup and started throwing snowballs for Bax, while Phoebe, who'd probably never played catch in her life, tried to get in on the action. The problem was, she had no idea what exactly the action was, and her comical antics, on top of Bax's continued confusion over the disappearing balls, had them howling with laughter.

When they went back inside, Elise started breakfast while Rohan dried off the dogs and then gave them their food and fresh water.

After his chore, he washed his hands at the sink, but his attention was completely focused on Elise. He couldn't help it. If they were in the same room, she was all he could see.

Even now he couldn't believe what had happened. In the space of two days, he had gone from closed-off loner to a father, head-over-heels in love with his child's mother. Or maybe besotted lover was a better description.

He felt lighter, freer and happier than he could ever remember being. It was like he'd been living in a twilight world for years, and then, suddenly there was light all around him.

Christmas lights, at this point. And carols playing on the stereo.

And he loved it all.

But he was still stressed about the meeting

between him and Jeevan, just as he knew Elise was, too.

Things might be wonderful between him and Elise, but Jeevan was still, to Rohan, an unknown quantity. Any number of things could go wrong. Jeevan could hate him, which would potentially put stress on the relationships between mother and son, and definitely between his parents.

Jeevan might be an adult, almost the same age Elise was when she gave birth, but he also was still Elise's main concern. And Rohan wouldn't want it any other way.

How would he react, should his son despise him? Would he be willing and able to give up the happiness he'd only just found with Elise, so as to not interfere with the bond between mother and son? Would she expect that of him?

"Hey," she said, pulling him out of his rambling, whirling thoughts. "It'll be okay."

"Yes," he replied and even nodded, although he wasn't at all sure.

"I have a hair appointment at two," she said, flipping pancakes on the griddle. "You can stay here if you want, or come into town with me."

"I'll go," he said, trying not to sound too eager. He'd planned to go to Banff later, to find her a Christmas gift, and this way she wouldn't be suspicious. "While you're getting your hair done, I can walk around and see the rest of the place."

After breakfast he helped her in the kitchen and then took down the boxes of ornaments from the attic. It was nothing exciting, but the peace he felt as the two of them worked together—the rightness of it—made him happier than he could have ever imagined.

Who would have thought something as normal as peeling and cutting up potatoes could feel like a benediction, when done in the right company?

The rest of the day passed in a blur, although when he thought about it, besides the trip into Banff they'd done nothing extraordinary. Yet before he knew it, it was time to shower and dress for the SAR fundraiser.

When he was ready, he sat in the living room waiting for Elise, and picked up the photo album once more. While looking at the images still brought pangs of regret for the time they'd lost, now they also reassured him that what was happening between them wasn't completely crazy.

The way they'd looked at each other clearly showed the love they'd felt, and he knew, although the memories were gone from his head, they'd somehow remained in his heart.

When he heard the tap of her heels coming

down the corridor, he closed the album and stood up, just as she came into the room.

Stunned, he stared, until she lifted a hand, self-consciously, to her throat.

"What?"

"You look gorgeous," he said, wondering if she'd agree to forgo the dinner so he could take his time exploring how to get her out of that red dress. "Everyone is going to hate me, for having the most beautiful woman in the room on my arm."

A tinge of rosy color stained her cheeks, and she smiled.

"Thank you. You're looking mighty fine yourself."

"Right now I want to kiss that lipstick right off those luscious lips, but I figure you'll beat me up if I did."

Her eyes got slumberous, and aforementioned lips came together in a sexy pout.

"I can always put more on," she said.

And that made them late leaving the house, because that was an invitation Rohan had no intention of passing up.

The hotel where the dinner was being held was decorated like a Christmas wonderland, and the ballroom was already full of people by the time they got there.

A tall, barrel-chested man came to meet them as they walked in, a relieved smile on his face.

"Elise. I thought you weren't coming."

"I told you I would be here, Tom," she said, tilting her cheek up for a kiss. "Let me introduce you. This is Dr. Rohan Khan. Rohan, Tom Harding, the head of the SAR team."

As they shook hands, Tom Harding gave Rohan a long, searching look.

"I heard that you went into that barn with Elise, to help bring Ben Sullivan out."

"Yes."

"Janice was so grateful to you both she called me from the hospital to tell me."

"I'm sorry I haven't filed a report yet, Tom," Elise interjected. "I haven't gotten around to it yet."

He waved his hand, as though brushing the words aside. "It's Christmas, so it can wait a few days, but I was wondering if Dr. Khan might be interested in volunteering for the team. We can always use another pair of hands."

Rohan shook his head. "I don't think it's in the cards for me, although I'm flattered you asked. Besides, I live in Calgary, so I wouldn't be of much help to you here."

"Shame," Tom said, sweeping his hand toward the front of the ballroom. "I was hoping you'd join and bring Elise back with you. She's one of the best we ever had."

"Actually, Tom, I wanted to talk to you about that."

Tom Harding's face lit up.

"You're ready to return? Put an end to this ridiculous retirement?"

"I'm thinking about it," she admitted. "But if you want me to handle a dog, I'll need a new one. I won't endanger Bax's health by putting him back in the field."

Tom rubbed his hands together, as though someone had just offered him a million dollars, and he was contemplating how to spend it.

"We'll talk about it, after we get all this holiday malarkey out of the way, but this is the best news I've had in weeks."

Elise laughed. "You've been just fine without me."

"But we're better with you." He glanced around as someone called his name, and then continued, "Go mix and mingle, and put in some bids. There's something special coming up in a few minutes, so listen out."

He hurried away, and Rohan realized he was beaming at Elise and couldn't seem to stop, even when she lifted her eyebrows, and asked, "Why are you grinning like that?"

Moving close to her side, he put his hand on her waist and bent to whisper in her ear.

"I'm just so damn proud of you right now."

Lifting her hand, she touched his scarred cheek, the gentle brush of her fingers making his heart sing.

"I wouldn't have found the courage without you."

Elise reveled in the moment with Rohan, so glad he was pleased with her decision to go back to the SAR team. It might have sounded spur-of-the-moment to him, but she'd found herself thinking about what he'd said about courage, and realized it was the right time to find hers.

She'd given up her dream out of fear but knew in her heart that she'd regret walking away from it forever.

After all, she might be on the other side of fifty, but there was a lot of good she could still do. And if the day came when she physically couldn't do the job anymore, that would be the time to retire. Not when she was still fit—and still wanted to be involved.

When he kissed her cheek, his lips lingering warm and tender against her skin, she also knew being with him was, as he'd intimated, her destiny.

That her love had never truly died but stayed

dormant in her heart, until he'd returned to awaken it again.

"I have to tell you something," she whispered, putting her palm on his cheek to keep him close.

"Go ahead," he said, equally softly, pulling back just far enough to see her eyes.

"I love you. I always have, and always will."

His face went blank for a moment, and her heart dipped, and then, before she could backtrack, he smiled, his entire face lighting up with love equal to her own.

"I love you, too," he said. "But couldn't you have waited just a little longer to tell me, so I wouldn't be tempted to embarrass you in front of all your colleagues?"

"No," she replied, stroking his cheek. "I've waited long enough."

He took a deep breath, his fingers tightening on her waist.

"Later, we'll discuss this in depth," he said, dark eyes gleaming, promising sweet retribution. "And I think I might need a demonstration, just to be sure you mean it."

Elise huffed a laugh, which was curtailed by the rush of desire melting her insides.

"Agreed, on both our parts," she said before stepping back. This really wasn't the place to grab him and kiss him, no matter how badly she wanted to. "Let's get something to drink, shall we? It's suddenly really warm in here."

He laughed and agreed, settling his hand at the base of her spine to guide her toward the bar.

As they strolled around the edge of the ballroom drinks in hand, looking at the auction items and bidding on a few, she was aware of the curious stares they were getting, but she didn't care. Soon enough it would be common knowledge that Jeevan's father was back in the picture, and back in her life.

Intimately.

Forever.

No one they spoke to was bold enough to ask any questions outright, which amused her no end, since she knew there were a few people there who probably were speculating.

Anyone who knew Jeevan, and most of the folks there did, would see the resemblance.

As they were talking to one of her former SAR colleagues, Kaylyn, and her husband, the PA system squawked, and they all looked up to see Tom at the podium.

He tapped the mike, then said, "Good evening, ladies and gentlemen. Thank you all for coming out tonight to support our annual Christmas fundraiser. In a little while we'll get dinner going, but tonight we're starting with a little surprise."

The crowd murmured, and Elise whispered to Kaylyn, "What's going on?"

When the other woman shrugged, Elise looked back at Tom.

"Last year, as you all know, we lost a valuable member of our team to retirement. Dr. Elise van Hagan was, and is, one of the finest and most valuable rescuers I've worked with in my career."

Shocked, Elise could hardly hear what Tom was saying, and when Rohan put his arm around her, she gladly leaned into his side, needing his support.

"When the committee met to plan this function, talk turned to how much we respected and admired Dr. van Hagan for her service. After surprisingly little debate, it was decided that tonight, we would honor her with a small token of our appreciation. Elise, would you come up here, please?"

"Go on," Rohan whispered as people started clapping. He took her glass from her hand and gave her a little nudge, when she didn't immediately move.

Reluctantly, but keeping her head high, Elise made her way to the small raised stage and then up the stairs. Tom was beaming at her and held out his hand to pull her close to the microphone.

"Elise, this was planned before you told me,

just this evening, that you're thinking of returning to our SAR team—"

He had to pause as applause broke out again, and wait until it faded before he could continue.

"That decision on your part is more welcome than you can ever imagine, but it doesn't detract from the amazing work you've done over the last ten years." He turned to the audience and said, "A couple of days ago, I called on Elise, asking her to go to the site of a barn collapse, because the team couldn't get there as quickly as she could. Without hesitation, she went, and saved a young man's life."

The applause was louder this time, with a few whistles thrown in, and Elise felt heat flow into her cheeks.

"Come on, Tom," she said pertly, giving him a smile, wanting off the stage. "Cut to the chase. I'm sure all these people are starving."

That drew laughter, even from Tom, who was shaking his head.

"Okay, then. The doctor has spoken. Elise, on behalf of the SAR team, and all the people you've saved over the last ten years, we'd like to present to you this plaque celebrating both your long service to the team, and to our community."

There were footsteps behind her, and she

turned, expecting the committee chairwoman or some other dignitary. Instead...

"Jeevan!"

His smile was wide, but she knew him well enough to see the question in his eyes. But none of that mattered as she threw her arms around him and he hugged her in return. The thunderous applause drowned out her words, but it didn't matter.

"You're home!"

CHAPTER NINETEEN

ROHAN STOOD ROOTED to the spot, staring at the man who'd walked out from the wings to surprise his mother. He couldn't stop the smile spreading across his face, and his heart was pounding. Thankful for the column beside him, he held on to it, needing something solid to lend support to his suddenly shaky legs.

My son!

As mother and son hugged, warmth flooded Rohan's chest, and they were all he could see.

There was so much love there he could hardly bear to watch. Elise had tears in her eyes, and Jeevan touched a finger to her cheek, laughing at her shock.

But then they both turned, in unison, and looked at him, and suddenly his joy was curtailed.

Jeevan might still be smiling for the crowd, but his eyes were flinty, interrogative.

He must have been watching from behind

the curtains and wondering who it was with his mother. And just like Elise when she first saw him, he hadn't recognized who it was.

The group walked off the stage, Tom still beaming, and disappeared behind the drapery flanking the opening.

What should he do now?

Go to them? Stay where he was?

The suddenness of Jeevan's appearance, the public nature of it, had his anxiety rising, and the urge to slip away almost overwhelmed him, but he stood his ground, waiting. The man who retreated from life, from emotions, took a distant second place to the father—and the lover—who would wait a lifetime to be with his family, if necessary.

Elise's head popped out from behind the curtain, and her gaze found his unerringly. There was no need for her to wave. Rohan was already moving, walking toward one of the most important and pivotal moments in his life.

His stomach was in knots and his mouth was dry, but nothing could stop him going to her, and his son.

"There never was an Australia trip. I planned to surprise you all along, with Tom's help," Rohan heard Jeevan say, as he walked up the steps to the stage. "Who's the guy? You look really into each other. Did he get you to go back to the SAR team?"

Rohan paused behind the curtain, suddenly unsure again and wishing he had the right to the kind of hug Jeevan had given his mother, full of love and joy.

"He's…" Elise caught sight of Rohan as he stepped fully out into her view, and her voice faltered to a stop.

Jeevan turned.

This close, Rohan could see how much they truly looked alike, and realized they were almost the same height, with his son an inch or so taller.

Rohan's heart was pounding so hard he felt almost light-headed, but he held his son's gaze, seeing his brow furrow and his mouth tighten.

"Mom?"

Elise seemed unable to move, to speak, and it was then that Rohan realized she'd been equally nervous about this moment.

"How this all came about is a long story, but I'm your father."

Jeevan turned to his mother and said again, "Mom?"

She was shaking, but she nodded and tried to smile. "It's true. He's alive, and he found us."

Jeevan faced Rohan again, the bewilderment in his eyes tearing at Rohan's heart.

"How… I thought… I thought you were dead."

"I'll explain it to you," Elise said, and her words pushed a rush of cold through Rohan's body.

Not we. But just her.

Yet wasn't that her prerogative? She'd raised Jeevan by herself, taken care of him and nurtured him into the man standing between them, looking from one to the other.

They had a relationship, while he—he was still the outsider looking in, hoping to be accepted.

"I'll let you two talk," he said, fighting to keep the coldness out of his voice, unable to stop his expression from going blank.

Some habits were harder to break than others.

He turned to go back to the ballroom.

"Wait."

Two voices, calling out at the same time, stopped him in his tracks, and he turned back to see Jeevan coming after him.

Then he was enveloped in a hug so tight he heard his ribs creak, but he didn't care, as Jeevan's voice, muffled but audible, said, "Dad. Daddy."

And when he hugged his son in return, everything felt right in the world.

Elise wasn't sure how she made it through the dinner, and the three of them left immediately afterward, needing time for Jeevan to sort through it all.

He peppered them with questions the entire way back to the house, stopping only for the time it took for him to go in and pick up his bags from his friend's house, where he'd been staying.

They had to go back to the beginning, explaining about the accident, and the way his grandfather had manipulated the story to get Elise out of Rohan's life.

"Wow," he remarked. "That was pretty low. Do you know why he did it?"

"I think, because he wanted me to marry a friend's daughter so the two families would be tied together. My father always was all about business and money, which equal prestige for some people."

"Yeah," he said. "I know some of them."

He was quiet for a moment, then asked, "Did you? Marry the woman your father wanted you to?"

"Yes, but it didn't work out."

Another brief silence, and when Elise looked in the rearview mirror, she saw Jeevan shaking his head.

"I'm sorry you went through that, Dad."

And her heart ached when Rohan lifted his hand to his face, not to touch his scars as he habitually did, but to swipe at his eyes.

"Thank you, son."

"Holy crap!" Jeevan's sudden shout almost made Elise drive off the road. "I have my dad back. Well, I have my dad." He laughed, and the joyful sound had her blinking back tears, too. Thank goodness she was pulling into the driveway. "Hey, Dad, wanna teach me how to throw a baseball?"

"Sorry, son." The amusement in Rohan's voice was apparent. "I grew up in Trinidad, so I could maybe teach you how to play cricket. But baseball? No. And don't even think about hockey."

The three of them were laughing as they got out of the car, and Elise had to stop for a moment, too thankful to move.

It would work out. She knew it would. And the relief was almost paralyzing.

"Come on, Mom," Jeevan said, putting his arm around her shoulder. "I'm sure there must be a butter tart with my name in the house somewhere. Otherwise, it just isn't Christmas."

"If your father hasn't eaten all of them," she replied, and on hearing her words, they all paused, as though letting them soak in.

Then Rohan said, "Hey, don't have him hating me already. At least let him get to know me first so his dislike is an honest one, not over baked goods."

"I've never hated you." Jeevan's voice had lost all mirth and was serious. Almost grave. "And I never will. So that part of the father-son bonding experience won't happen."

"Glad to hear it," Rohan said. Then, as though unable to help themselves, they hugged again.

Baxter went wild when Jeevan walked in, scaring Phoebe in the process. By the time Rohan and Jeevan had them both settled down, Elise had made hot chocolate, and they went into the living room to drink it.

When Jeevan saw that the tree wasn't decorated, he insisted they get on it. It couldn't be bare on Christmas morning.

"You should write a book." Jeevan considered where on the tree to put the glittery ornament he was holding, then reached up and hung it on the topmost bough, before looking at his father. "It's like a soap opera, or a Bollywood movie.

The hero is dead, and then, when you least expect it, he isn't."

When Rohan laughed, Elise felt now familiar warmth fill her chest. She would never tire of hearing that sound.

"When you put it that way, sure. But no one would believe it actually happened. They'd think I made it up."

Elise nodded her agreement as she hunted for some more ornament wires. Every year she misplaced them and ended up buying more. They should be drowning in them by now. If she didn't know he was too well trained to do something like that, she'd think Baxter was hiding them somewhere.

"People nowadays wouldn't understand what it was like when it was all landlines, and local newspapers and TV. You hardly knew what was happening one town over, much less a thousand miles away," she said. "Now everyone has a cell phone with video capabilities, and are posting selfies all over the internet, and even the smallest countries have their newspapers online. Anyone who didn't live before the worldwide web would think it was the most ridiculous story they'd ever heard."

Jeevan obviously was still trying to make sense of it all, and Elise knew it would take some more time. But when she'd seen him spontaneously hug Rohan, she'd known it would be all right in the end.

They still hadn't broached the subject of his parents being together again, after having reconnected only a couple of days ago. She and Rohan had already agreed that, for at least these first few nights, they'd sleep apart. One shock at a time was enough for their son.

Yet she didn't really want to wait. Not now, when Rohan and her had admitted to their feelings. She was chomping at the bit to start the rest of their life together, as a couple, as well as a family.

"Gosh, I love Christmas." The contentment in Jeevan's voice mirrored the feeling that blossomed in her chest as she watched the two most important people in her life interact so easily. "And this year is the best ever."

"I can't wait to hear all about your trip to Indonesia and Borneo." Rohan handed Elise a plastic bag filled with the wires she'd been hunting for. "Did you get enough data for your doctorate?"

"Yes, I'm sure I did. It was amazing there, but rough living most of the time. I can understand why some scientists only want to do field work, but jungle living isn't for me. At least not all the time."

As the two men talked more about the trip, Elise allowed herself a little moment of relief. She'd been worried Jeevan might decide that adventures in faraway places suited him perfectly and then end up living in inaccessible locales all the time. Hearing him say it wasn't for him made her happy, even though she knew he wouldn't stay in Banff.

For now, she was perfectly content with what she had, and knew she shouldn't be greedy. No matter where Jeevan settled, they'd still be in touch, and visit regularly. At least, she'd visit him regularly, whether he wanted it or not. When she was ninety and he was sixty-three, he'd still be her baby. And Rohan would still be the love of her life.

Christmas had definitely taken on a new sparkle. Where before she'd associated it with loss, now it had become what it was always meant to be: a season of hope and joy and love.

"Were you the one who encouraged Mom to go back to SAR?" Jeevan asked Rohan. "I've been telling her for the past year that she shouldn't give it up. Do you know she passed the physical at forty-two, and some of the people half her age flunked it?"

Rohan gave her a look that heated her to her toes, and she was glad Jeevan was once more deciding where to hang an ornament, and not focused on them.

"I didn't know that, but I'm not surprised. And no, I didn't encourage her, per se, just told her I thought she was amazing at it."

And that led to them telling their son about the joint rescue they'd effected, and their being on site to help Mrs. Pilar, when she collapsed in Banff, as well as the raven they'd rescued.

"You guys have been busy, eh?"

"You could say that," she replied.

The tree was almost completely decorated when Jeevan turned to his father and said, "It just struck me—you told Mom you'd be back for Christmas, but it took you twenty-seven years to keep your promise." Jeevan quirked an eyebrow at his father. "I guess better late than never."

"I'm a man of my word," Rohan said with mock gravity. "Just a little tardy sometimes."

They exchanged almost identical grins, which they turned on Elise, making her heart ache with happiness. Her eyes got damp and she smiled back, shaking her head at their silliness. Mind you, she might as well get used to it. They were more alike than not, and she could almost bet they'd be ganging up on her sometimes. She resolved to stay on her toes, and ready for anything.

"I still think you could have a bestseller on your hands," Jeevan said, sending his parents another teasing glance. "And if you cap the story off by getting married, then you could tap into the romance market. I hear it's huge."

"Jeevan!"

Elise put as much outrage as she could into her voice, but Rohan completely spoiled the effect by muttering, "Hush, son. Don't spook her. I'm working on it."

"Definitely the best Christmas ever," Jeevan said happily.

"The first of many."

The surety and love in Rohan's voice was patent, and Elise got up from her chair to lean down and kiss him lightly, no longer concerned with how Jeevan might interpret her actions. He obviously already knew his parents were back in love and had no problem with it.

There would no doubt be more discussions about everything, later. But right now, she had to express all the love in her heart.

Rohan pulled her down into his lap and, under Jeevan's teasing gaze, wrapped both arms around her waist.

"Yes," she agreed, snuggling in, at home again in Rohan's embrace, contentment making her smile. "The first of many merry Christmases. Together."

* * * * *

*If you enjoyed this story, check out
these other great reads from
Ann McIntosh*

Best Friend to Doctor Right
Awakened by Her Brooding Brazilian
The Nurse's Christmas Temptation
Surgeon Prince, Cinderella Bride

All available now!